THE TROOPER'S TREASURE

CONTEMPORARY CHRISTIAN ROMANCE

FULLER FAMILY IN BRUSH CREEK ROMANCE
BOOK THREE

LIZ ISAACSON

ISBN-13: 978-1638760894

"Repent ye therefore, and be converted, that your sins may be blotted out, when the times of refreshing shall come from the presence of the Lord."

Acts 3:19

Chapter 1

Dawn Fuller couldn't stop her foot from bouncing. Her knee went up-down, up-down, up-down over and over, increasing in rate and intensity with every passing second. She kept her eyes on the ground so her hair would fall over her shoulders and hide her face.

The horrible scent of rubbing alcohol and the stringency of other medical products assaulted her, and she couldn't wait to get out of the women's clinic. Her stomach roiled, and she hoped it was all from nerves, that the test she'd just taken would be negative.

Though she was definitely living up to her label as the "wild child" of the Fuller family, she couldn't imagine walking into her conservative parent's home and telling them she was pregnant.

Only twenty-six and without a husband—or even a

boyfriend anymore—Dawn simply couldn't fathom bringing a child into the world and attempting to raise it.

Please, she prayed, though she felt like a complete loser for lifting her voice to the Lord. *Please let it be negative.* She wasn't sure what God could do now. He was all-powerful, but he couldn't un-make a baby that would've been conceived seven weeks ago.

Dawn pressed her eyes closed, her desperation surging up her throat and making her gag. How long did it take to read a pregnancy test? She'd been waiting for at least ten minutes, or so she thought. Since she'd suspected she was pregnant, every minute felt like a lifetime.

"Dawn Fuller?"

Her eyes snapped open and she stood like she'd been shot out of a cannon. "Here." She cursed herself for practically yelling like she was in school and needed to be marked present. She approached the curly-haired woman wearing pink scrubs, her feet like lead and her heart thundering in her chest.

"Here you go, sweetie." She handed her a sealed envelope and looked past Dawn like the slip of paper inside wouldn't be life-changing. Yes or no, whatever the test said, Dawn's whole life would change.

"Tara?" the nurse called, and Dawn slipped out of the women's center and back to her car. It took all her courage to slide her fingers under the flap of the envelope and rip it open. She pulled out a single third-sheet of paper that had a bunch of letters on it Dawn didn't understand.

She did, however, understand what NEGATIVE meant.

Sobs shook her shoulders, her body, and she crumpled over the steering wheel with gratitude and relief shattering through her. After the storm had blown itself out, she straightened, pushed her hair off her face, and looked out the windshield.

Drawing in a deep breath, she tried to settle herself. She needed to make the one-hour drive back to Brush Creek before she was missed.

She scoffed at herself. "No one even knows you're gone." She started the car to get the air conditioning going, and set herself north and west along the two-lane highway. She'd gone a couple of miles when her tears hit her again.

Thankfully, there wasn't anyone out here in the middle of the day, and if her car went over the center line a couple of times, it was fine. She loved driving fast in the middle of nowhere, and the soft roar of the wind as her two-seater cut through the atmosphere helped to calm her.

She glanced down at her speedometer and realized she was driving just a bit too fast, even for her. Easing up on the accelerator, she focused back out the windshield again. Movement caught her eye, and she slammed on the brakes as a deer bounded in front of her car.

Dawn screamed, yanked the wheel to the right as the deer went left, and watched in slow motion as her car left the road and soared into the ditch.

She braced for impact, her fingers so tight against the steering wheel. The deafening sound of bending metal on scrunching metal tore through her ears. The car came to a stop and steam rose from the hood, obscuring her view.

Dawn breathed, her adrenaline so high she could barely do much more than basic bodily functions. Pain cascaded through her body, stemming from her leg. Glancing down, she found her calf stuck between the crumpled metal and the seat. Blood stained her shorts and dripped down to her shoeless foot.

Her stomach lurched. She'd never been able to stand the sight of her own blood and a whiteness covered her vision.

She tried to pull her leg out, but it was stuck. She tried to open the door, but that was stuck too. The air conditioning blew hot air now, making it hard to inhale. Panic built inside her, and she needed to get out of this car. Now.

Her fingers scrabbled for something. Something to let her out.

A moan came from her mouth, building into a scream. She pounded against the window, her gaze falling to her leg. The air left her body. She couldn't pass out here. No one knew where she was.

"Phone," she moaned, but she had no idea where her purse was. She tried the door again, to no avail.

The mania inside her faded to nothing, and she slumped against the headrest. She touched her leg, and her fingers came away sticky. Her stomach swooped, and she welcomed the unconsciousness as it swept toward her.

"Hold on!" someone yelled through the glass, and Dawn had enough energy to open her eyes and look out the window. But the gorgeous, mature face of McDermott Boyd was the last man she wanted to see.

She moaned again as the handsome State Trooper hurried around the back of the car to the passenger door. He ripped it open and peered inside. "Are you—?" He blinked, his dark eyes registering his surprise and delight. "Dawn?"

Dawn let her head flop to the opposite side. She didn't want McDermott to see her like this. Didn't want to explain anything to him. She'd grown up with the Boyd family, and though McDermott was a Brush Creek native too, it was his little brothers that were Dawn's age.

No matter what, he knew what kind of woman she was. *What kind of woman you used to be*, she told herself as he pulled her across the seat.

She screamed as white hot pain shot through her, and she looked into McDermott's panicked and concerned face before she blacked out completely.

———

THE NEXT TIME SHE WOKE, the smell of toast met her nose. Whoever had put bread in the toaster and slathered it with butter really knew her. "Mom?" She tried to push herself up and found her left leg achy, but bandaged.

"Leave her be," a man said in a soft, pleasant voice, and Dawn's eyes flew to the sliver of light coming from the doorway. "Go on, now. Go see what Nana Reba wants you to do for dinner."

The pitter of little feet sounded, and then McDermott opened the door holding a plate of toast and a glass of something she hoped was orange juice.

"Hey, you're awake." He set the food on the bedside table and switched on the lamp there. "We're at my house." He chuckled and jostled his powerful shoulders in a squirmy sort of shrug. "Well, it's my Nana Reba's house, but we live here." He sat in an armchair in the corner, near the foot of the bed. "Me and my daughter. We live here with her." He seemed to realize that he'd started rambling a bit, and he pressed his mouth into a thin line.

"What happened?" Her head ached and she touched her forehead. There were no memories there. How in the world had she gotten to McDermott Boyd's house? Why had he brought her toast? Why was her leg injured?

"You don't remember?"

She sifted through the soft thoughts in her head. "I... don't remember."

"What's the last thing you do remember?" He still wore his trooper uniform, but had discarded the hat so she could see his dark hair that he kept cropped close to his scalp.

"I, uh...." Dawn leaned back against the headboard. "I was in Vernal."

He nodded, his eyes never leaving hers. The light was too dim to read too much into his expression, but Dawn didn't like the appraising way he watched her. She felt like he was more cop in the moment than an old friend.

She didn't want to be friends with him anyway. He was a perfect gentleman, a great dad, and a widower who'd lost his wife in the worst way possible. She was a complete wreck of a human being, and she could barely look at him without a river of shame tumbling through her.

Dawn closed her eyes to block out his handsome features. "I don't remember anything after that."

"You don't know what you were doing in Vernal?" He must be able to get people to tell him anything with a honeyed voice like that.

"I can't remember."

"Well." He sighed and she imagined him stretching his long legs out in front of him. "You were driving back from something in Vernal, and a deer ran across the road. You braked to miss it, swerved, and went into the ditch."

Dawn's eyes popped open. "And you saw that?"

"I sure did. I was about a half a mile behind you and I saw you go off the road." His right eyebrow quirked. "You were driving pretty fast."

Dawn didn't remember that, but she did like to

speed in general, so she didn't contradict him. "You brought me back to your house?"

"You asked me to."

It was her turn to quirk her eyebrows, and she even added a scoff. "I don't think—"

"I pulled you out of the car, and you passed in and out of consciousness. I asked you if you needed to go to the hospital, and you begged me not to take you." He looked over to the door as it opened. "C'mon, baby. You can come in."

A blonde angel skipped into the room and went over to her father. She leaned into him, shy and forward at the same time.

McDermott looked at Dawn but didn't introduce his daughter. "She wanted to make you toast. So we'll leave you to rest and eat. I had your car towed to Mick's, so I'll drive you home whenever you want." He took his daughter's hand and led her out of the room, the doe-eyed child still silent as she went with her dad.

As soon as the door snicked closed, Dawn swung her legs over the side of the bed. The toast, once appetizing, was cold now, and she needed to get out of this room, this house, before she allowed that beautiful man to care for her.

"He already has," she muttered to herself. The thought that he'd be interested in her beyond making sure she got home safe was laughable. In any case, Dawn wasn't interested. Not anymore. She needed to get her life together before she could even think about bringing someone else into it.

But if you were ready, she thought as she stood and tested her weight on her injured leg. *Maybe you should take a closer look at McDermott.*

CHAPTER 2

McDermott fully expected Dawn to come out of the spare bedroom within ten minutes. It took her seven. He stood from the couch where Nana Reba had turned on a movie about ponies and magic for Taya.

"I'm ready," Dawn said.

McDermott plucked a ball cap from the hat rack next to the front door and went to help her. Of course he knew Dawn Fuller. He'd grown up with the Fuller boys, and Kyler was his best friend all through high school. Dawn was several years younger, but so beautiful now that she was all grown up that McDermott's thoughts were going in a dozen directions.

He put his hand on the back of her elbow, and a zing shot into his shoulder. Oh, boy. He wondered if she felt it too, or if he was being overly sensitive because it had been traumatic to see that car go careening into a ditch earlier that afternoon.

"The first step is big," he said in a quiet voice as he pushed open the door and let her go first. "Be back in a few minutes, Nana. Taya, you can stay up until I get back." He held onto her all the way to the car. Since it was still spring, it was already dark though it was only eight o'clock.

"You sure you're okay?" he asked once she was settled and he'd started the car. "You don't need to go to the hospital?"

"There isn't one here anyway," she said. "And I'm not going back to Vernal." She clenched her arms around her midsection, and McDermott could read body language better than most. "I live above the bookstore."

Case closed, he thought. He put the car in drive and eased out of the driveway. The silence between them felt full of awkwardness, so he said, "How's Brennan doing in California?"

"Fine."

"The wedding was nice, even if they had to move it to the fire station."

"Yep."

McDermott cut her a look out of the corner of his eye as they passed under an orange street lamp. She seemed like she'd probably be okay if he left her alone tonight. Still, something nagged at him, and he hoped he wouldn't come off as a creeper.

He pulled into the bookstore parking lot and peered at the building. "Here?"

"My door is around to the left."

McDermott steered his cruiser over there and sure enough, a door sat there he'd never used. Not that he went to the bookstore that often in the first place. He put the car in park and the locks released.

"So I'd feel more comfortable if I knew you weren't going to be alone," he said. "Do you live with someone? A roommate?"

She swiveled her head toward him, her sky-blue eyes searching his. "No. I live alone."

"I'm worried you might have a concussion. Or need help." He looked at the door. "Can you call one of your siblings? Your parents?"

Dawn looked at him like *stop being such a cop*, but he couldn't help it. "I'm fine, McDermott."

"So you'll call someone in your family if you need help. I'd feel better—"

"I'm not calling one of them."

Surprise moved through him, but he kept his face completely placid. "Would you like my number so you can call me?"

She snorted and started laughing, quieting quickly when he continued staring at her. "Oh, you're serious."

"I'm serious," he confirmed. "You went head-first into a ditch. I got you out quick, and your leg just had a flesh wound. I watched you for signs of a concussion and didn't see any, but I'm worried about you being alone."

"Fine." She made a big show of rifling through her purse and pulling out her phone. She practically slapped it into his palm, but he'd dealt with a lot of difficult people in his twelve years working for the Utah Highway Patrol.

He put his number into her phone and handed it back. "All right. Let's get you upstairs."

"I can manage."

He chuckled as he unbuckled. "Wow, you're really trying to be alone, aren't you?" He went around and met her at the door, where she had the key nearly in the lock.

She opened the door and looked up at him, angry fire in her eyes. "I like being alone."

McDermott tucked an errant curl behind her ear. "Oh, sweetheart. I can tell a lie when I hear one." He nodded toward the tall staircase. "Want me to carry you? That's a lot of steps."

Her teeth ground together and she said, "You are not carrying me." Shuffling into the building, she started up the stairs, one at a time. He stayed behind her in case she lost her balance, and they navigated to her apartment one painfully slow step at a time.

Her door wasn't locked, and she turned in the open doorway. "Thank you, McDermott. I'm clearly safe and inside my apartment. There are no more stairs. You can go."

At least she'd said thank you. But McDermott didn't want to go. He forced himself to back away from her, lift one hand in a goodbye wave, and watch as she practically slammed the door in his face.

A chuckle started in his chest as he pounded down the steps and went back to his cruiser. Dawn Fuller was a feisty one, and her reputation as the wild child Fuller certainly seemed true. He hoped her memory would come back soon enough, and he hoped he'd be able to run into her around the police department.

He often did, as she cleaned the building late in the evening and he sometimes went back to his office after Taya went to bed. As he slowly drove home, he realized how Dawn had cropped up in his life over the years.

"Maybe she'd go out with you," he mused as he scanned Oxbow Park as if he was on duty. As if Oxbow Park was even under his jurisdiction, which it wasn't.

He'd had a rough time getting a date since his wife's death, mostly because he hadn't tried until recently. It had been so long since he'd looked around town for a date, that he didn't realize how slim the choices were. So many of his former classmates had left town or gotten married, and there weren't a whole lot of eligible women in town his age.

Dawn was six years younger than him.... "But she's beautiful," he said to himself again. "What would it hurt to try?"

But he knew what it would hurt. His heart. His daughter. And probably a whole lot of other things McDermott didn't even know about yet. But he was tired of sleeping alone. He wasn't really alone, as he had

Taya and Nana Reba, as well as his parents who still lived in town. But he didn't confide in them the way he had Amelia.

He wanted a best friend, a lover, a soul mate to help him raise his daughter. He sighed as he pulled into Nana Reba's driveway and saw the lamplight in the windows.

"Thank you for bringing me home safe tonight," he whispered to the Lord, the same way he did every night when he made it back to his daughter alive. After all, he knew that sometimes cops didn't come home safe at night.

Amelia hadn't. And he couldn't bear the thought of Taya being an orphan. So he prayed each morning for safety, and expressed his gratitude each evening he got to come home and hug his daughter tight.

———

"Go on and get your boots." McDermott glanced at Taya, who sat at the bar like a princess waiting to be served. "Nana's almost done with the eggs. Then we'll eat and go."

"Can I ride Cinnamon today?"

"You'll have to ask Walker." He turned as the toast popped up. "Now go on. We're already runnin' late." He buttered toast as Nana Reba scooped eggs onto plates. He poured juice, enjoying the warmth in the house, the hustle and bustle of family life on a weekend morning, and feeling a measure of peace that had been elusive the past few weeks.

"It's cold today," Nana Reba said in her creaky old voice as she opened the sliding glass door to let in the dogs. Thelma and Louise, golden retriever sisters, nearly trampled each other as they came in. Nana Reba closed the door and laughed. "You two. You're menaces. Go on now. Go on! I'll get your eggs."

Thelma and Louise were McDermott's dogs, but Nana Reba had taken quite the liking to them. She'd made enough eggs for them to each have a bowl, and she made them sit and wait while she set their food on their mats. "All right," she finally said, and the dogs attacked the food, nearly knocking Nana Reba down in the process.

McDermott couldn't help smiling. Just because life wasn't exactly the way he wanted it, or the way he'd imagined it when he'd married Amelia and they'd had Taya, didn't mean it wasn't still wonderful.

Taya came back into the kitchen, her white-blonde hair wisping around her face. After Amelia's death, doing Taya's hair had been one of McDermott's greatest challenges. He often thought of his late wife while he brushed and braided, as it was something Amelia always did, no exceptions.

"Let's pray," he said. "The eggs are gettin' cold. You say it, baby."

As his angel daughter's voice blessed the food and asked for them to be safe while they went horseback riding, McDermott's heart melted. He was trying to be a good father, but he worked a lot. Taya would start first grade in the fall, and some of his guilt would be alleviated then. No matter what he did, though, he knew he couldn't be both a mom and a dad.

"Amen," she said, and McDermott echoed her before rounding the island and sitting on a stool that felt like it wouldn't hold his weight.

"What are you doin' today, Nana?" he asked.

"Going up to the strawberry fields."

McDermott nodded. "Does Mom need any more help?"

"She can always use more help in the spring." Nana took a drink of her orange juice. "But don't worry about coming. You guys go do your riding and then relax. It's supposed to warm up by this afternoon."

"Maybe the pool will be open," Taya said.

"Hon, the pool doesn't open until Memorial Day," McDermott said. He'd told her that at least half a dozen times. "One more week, baby."

One more week, and school would be out too. One more week, and summer would be upon them. One more week. McDermott had endured a lot of things by telling himself to get through one more week.

"You can set the sprinkler under the trampoline," Nana said. "Or come up to the fields. I'm sure your grandma would love to see you."

McDermott stuffed a huge bite of toast into his mouth as a sliver of guilt gutted him. He lived with his maternal grandmother, so she got to see Taya all the time. She picked Taya up after kindergarten, fed her lunch, and took care of her all afternoon. Sure, she sometimes took her over to McDermott's parent's house, but they spent so much time working the eighty acres of strawberry fields they owned, that he usually made an effort to take Taya over on the weekends. He simply hadn't felt like it for a few weeks, because his mother always asked him when he was going to start dating again.

Dawn's face flashed before his eyes, and he pushed away his plate of cold eggs. He wanted to ask her out, but she hadn't given him her number. All he could do was hope she contacted him. Or he could run over to the office tonight, though he wasn't on duty today.

Or you could stop by her house to see if she's all right….

"You're not going to finish those?" Nana Reba's voice cut through his thoughts, and a hint of embarrassment crept through him. She couldn't see his thoughts, but sometimes it felt like she could.

"No, I'm full," he said, standing. "I'll get our jackets, Tay. Then it's time to go."

Properly fed and clothed, he whipped Taya's hair into a ponytail and they headed out in his cruiser for the horse farm up the hill from town. He'd known the previous owners, before Landon Edmunds had bought the place and turned it into a thriving ranch that produced rodeo horses.

McDermott had grown up with horses, but he didn't have the land or lifestyle to maintain them now. When

Walker Thompson had moved to town eight years ago, the two men had become fast friends. And when Amelia had died, McDermott had turned to Walker—a widower with a child himself—for advice, comfort, and friendship.

Taya loved running through the fields, riding horses, and playing with the assortment of dogs and children at the farm. When they showed up on Saturday mornings, McDermott felt like his soul had come home.

His tires crunched over the gravel, easing to a stop outside the middle cabin where Walker now lived with his wife and their two kids. Both Tess and Walker sat on the front porch, their knees almost to their chins, holding hands.

Taya flew from the backseat of the cruiser, Thelma and Louise not far behind. With many wagging tails—as Walker had two dogs of his own—the fun started. McDermott got out of the car a little slower, giving himself a stern talking-to not to mention Dawn Fuller.

Tess had been trying to set McDermott up for most of the past three years. And sure enough, the first thing she said after standing to embrace him was, "How do you feel about a stylist?"

He blinked at her. "I'm not sure what that is."

She giggled and swatted his bicep. "You do too. You know, a woman who cuts hair."

"Oh, uh...."

"Leave him be," Walker said, standing and putting

one arm around McDermott's shoulders in a manly hug. "Who wants to ride Cinnamon today?"

"I do!" Taya squealed, dodged one of the retrievers and skipped toward Walker. He scooped her up, causing her to laugh, and McDermott's heart expanded ten sizes.

"I've got cookies inside," Tess said, ducking through the doorway.

"Triple chocolate chip," Walker said, smiling. "They're my favorite."

"Daddy says I can start learning how to cook," Taya said.

"Is that right?" Walker asked. "What are you going to make?"

"I made toast last night," Taya said. "There was this woman who was passed out, and—"

"Taya," McDermott said, his heart rate spiking.

Her innocent blue eyes landed on his much darker ones. "Oh. I wasn't supposed to tell about her, huh?"

McDermott shook his head. "Not your business to tell." He met Walker's eyes, and he knew he'd be telling the story about Dawn Fuller before he left the farm. But not in front of Taya. His six-year-old didn't need to know about his crush on a woman who would barely look at him.

Dawn looked down at her phone as she finished washing her hands in the church kitchen. It darkened before she could catch who had texted.

She'd been cleaning the church pro bono for eleven months, something that soothed her soul and made her feel good about herself at least once a week.

The past year had been hard. Good. But hard. She felt like she'd made huge strides in some areas—like cleaning up her lifestyle, recommitting herself to following God's commandments, and putting in a good, honest day's work.

But in other areas, she felt like she had so far to go. She'd been working with Pastor Peters for months, and he'd said a few weeks ago that he thought she was done. But she still didn't like herself much. She still didn't include other people in her life—not even her family. And the loneliness seemed ever-present.

But she didn't want to hang out with her old friends. They had all the bad habits she'd worked so hard to eradicate. Making new friends had proven extremely difficult, as friends shared things with each other, and she didn't want to tell anyone about her past mistakes.

As far as she was concerned, they were between her, God, and Pastor Peters, and he'd said she was all right.

Dawn felt all right about her year of spiritual progress. There were so many things still lacking, though.

Her phone brightened again, this time flashing McDermott Boyd's name. "Oh, come on," she muttered as she dried her hands. He'd asked her out at least once a month for the past year. A whole year!

She'd put him off every time. Though he was handsome, and kind, and employed, and about a dozen other things Dawn liked, she simply didn't want to get involved with him. Number one, he'd grown up with her older brother. The stories Kyler could tell him about her made Dawn's skin crawl. Number two, he had a six-year-old daughter. Dawn didn't want a family—or a husband for that matter. And how arrogant of her to think she could just waltz into a child's life and be her mother? Or that McDermott even wanted a serious relationship with her?

Dawn didn't want serious, that was for certain. She wasn't good at short-term either, so she'd set a no-dating policy and stuck with it for twelve months.

She picked up her phone, thinking of the third strike

against McDermott: he'd been married before to a beautiful, wonderful woman that Dawn could never measure up to. Surely he wasn't interested in her, so why did he keep asking her out?

She tapped out, *I can't*, to his invitation to the weekend's concert in the park and sent the message. She never expanded on why she couldn't. He never asked. He'd wait a few weeks and invite her to something else. The worst was when he caught her in the police department and asked her out right to her face, right on the spot.

Her phone rang, and McDermott's name and face came up. Her breath stuck in her lungs at his handsomeness, and that alone prompted her to answer the call. "Hey," she said.

"Hey, yourself." His deep, delicious voice sent tremors through her. So maybe she'd fantasized about saying yes to him. But it would have to be in another lifetime, when she hadn't accumulated so many secrets— and he hadn't been married and started a family already.

"So real quick," he said. "I know you just said you couldn't go to the concert this weekend." He cleared his throat, and Dawn found it cute the he seemed nervous to talk to her. Her! If he had any idea what kind of person she really was....

"I'm just wondering what it will take to get you to go out with me."

Dawn's breath left her body. "Oh," she managed to say.

"You don't seem to like going to dinner. Or concerts.

Or picnics. I'm easy," he said. "I'll do whatever you want."

Getting some of her nerves under control, Dawn cocked her hip and asked, "Why do you keep asking?"

"Well, I figured that part's obvious."

"Not to me."

He coughed this time, the sound morphing into a choke. "Kyler says you're not seein' anyone," he said, like that should explain it all. Dawn bristled that sure enough, McDermott had spoken to her older brother.

"I'm not," she confirmed. "And I don't—"

"I think you're beautiful," McDermott said over the top of her. "And I think we'd get along real nice. And even when I go out with other women, I just keep comin' back to you." He spoke in a slow, measured cadence, his voice flowing through her ears like silk.

She sat heavily in the back row of the chapel, her legs unable to support her weight as *you're beautiful* rang through her head. He really thought so?

Just physically, she told herself. If he could see what was on the inside, he wouldn't think so.

Still, she found herself saying, "All right, McDermott. I'll go out with you."

"Yeah?"

"Yeah." It was as if someone else had taken control of Dawn's body. She couldn't believe she'd just agreed to a date with dreamy McDermott Boyd. The very fact that she found him dreamy and desirable sent up big red flags in her mind.

"So no to the concert," he said. "Maybe you'd like to go up to the horse farm and go horseback riding. Or out to the strawberry fields and do the you-pick. Somewhere away from the crowds."

So he wanted to hide their date from the public. Of course he did. He was a huge public figure in Brush Creek. The standard for well-groomed, educated, clean men everywhere.

"Or we can wait a couple of weeks and go to the balloon launch."

"That's at the rec center."

"Yeah." A skin of confusion hid in his voice. "So what?"

"So a lot of people will see us there."

Several beats of silence came through the line before he said, "And you don't want to be seen with me."

"No," she said quickly. "Try the other way around."

"What? Dawn, I'd be happy to be seen with you." He cleared his throat again.

"Then why'd you suggest somewhere without a crowd?"

"You seem adverse to them, that's all," he said. "I was trying to suggest somewhere you'd feel more comfortable."

Foolishness raced through Dawn. She should be used to the feeling by now, as she'd had to face a lot of foolish mistakes she'd made in her life while she worked through her past with Pastor Peters.

Scratching came through the phone, and she heard

the low murmur of McDermott's voice as he said something to his daughter. Dawn's fear spiked, and she almost hung up the phone. But Pastor Peters's voice was there, inside her head, telling her to lift up her chin and do what was right. That God would never turn her away for trying to make things right.

"Will Taya be coming on the date?" she asked.

"Well...no."

"Maybe I should meet her." Her mind spun. She absolutely didn't want to meet McDermott's child. She didn't want children. Where had that idea come from?

"You want to meet her-meet her? Like you're my girlfriend or something?" The incredulity in his voice sounded like a gong in Dawn's ears.

She sighed, her worry now that she was about to vomit up a lot of things she'd hoped to keep to herself for a good long while. "I'm scared of you," she blurted out. "You come with a previous wife and a kid and I'm—I'm not...."

Seconds passed. Maybe a full minute. Dawn wasn't sure how to finish the sentence she'd started, but it was clear McDermott was waiting for her to do just that.

"I don't think I'm ready for any of that."

"I'm not in a hurry," he said.

"That's why I've turned you down for a year," she continued as if he hadn't spoken. "I just think you're way out of my league, and—"

His laughter silenced her and sent another vein of foolishness through her.

"I am not out of your league, Dawn."

Oh, but he was. So far out of her league, he didn't even know it.

"I'll go anywhere and do anything you want," he added. "You name it, and I'll be there. If you want to meet Taya, that's fine too."

Dawn closed her eyes and prayed to know what the right thing was. "How about just dinner?" she asked. "Just you and me. There's a great restaurant in Beaverton called Parker's Lionhouse. We can…talk." She shook her head at her stupidity. Of course they'd have to talk.

"I know Parker's. That sounds fine."

"Fine."

"Tonight? Tomorrow? You work evenings, don't you?"

"I can do the bank cleaning in the afternoon on Saturdays," she said. "So Saturday would probably be best."

"Two days from now, Saturday? Or…?"

She just wanted him to make a decision. "Sure. Two days from now Saturday."

"Great." She could hear the smile in his voice. "I'm so glad I called. I'll pick you up around six?"

"Six is fine." Dawn's exhaustion forced her eyes closed again.

"See you then." He hung up, and Dawn let her hand fall to the pew, almost dropping her phone in the process.

"What have I just agreed to?" she said aloud. She opened her eyes and looked at the beautiful stained glass window at the front of the chapel. "Is this really the right thing to do?"

The sun shone right through the Lord's eye, making it twinkle as if He was saying, *If you always do what you've always done, you'll never get a different result.*

So she'd give McDermott a chance. A date. "Maybe two dates," she said, still watching the sun shine through the colored glass. And maybe, just maybe, she wouldn't be so lonely anymore.

————

DAWN TOOK a deep breath and faced the nondescript door. It led to an unremarkable office. Where her oldest sister, Wren, would be sitting behind a chest-high counter, probably playing solitaire on the computer.

"Just go in," she told herself for the fifth time. It wasn't that she had anything against Wren. The two women just happened to be polar opposites, what with Wren being the picture of perfection and all that. And Dawn...well, Dawn sat on the other end of perfect.

She pushed open the door anyway. Said, "Hey, Wren," at the same time her sister looked up. She jumped from her seat—well, she tried to. Being seven months pregnant and petite meant Wren couldn't really jump anywhere.

"Dawn." She wore a perfect smile as if she really was happy to see Dawn, and came around the counter to hug her. "What brings you in? You didn't get my text this morning?"

"No, I got it." Dawn held onto Wren for a breath too long, something her perceptive sister noticed.

She held onto Dawn's shoulders as she stepped back and looked at her. "So this isn't a problem with the job."

"No."

"It's personal."

Dawn had never been happier that Wren seemed to know everything, something that usually annoyed her to no end. "I, uh...." She cleared her throat. "I have a date, and I need your help getting ready for it."

Wren's blue eyes, a shade or two darker than Dawn's, widened, and a smile bloomed on her pretty face. "A date? It's about time!" She bustled around the counter and started clicking on the computer. "When is it?" She glanced up, her expression horrified now. "It's not tonight, is it? I mean, it's three-thirty already. I suppose you might have something to wear, but—"

"It's on Saturday." Maybe she could get away with not telling Dawn who she was going out with.

"Saturday. Okay, Saturday's doable."

Glad Wren thought so.

"Who's it with?" she asked, abandoning the computer now.

Dawn looked away from her sister. "Uh, McDermott Boyd."

Wren sat back in her chair as if Dawn had pushed her. "McDermott—Boyd—wow."

"Don't be so surprised," Dawn said, starting to regret coming here for help.

"You've rejected him for over a year," Wren said. "Why shouldn't I be surprised?"

"Not *over* a year," Dawn protested. It had been exactly a year since her car crash just last week. He didn't start asking her out until a few weeks after that.

"He's very good looking," Wren said, bringing the smile back.

"Exactly why I need help." Dawn leaned on the counter next to her keyboard. "I'm okay with my hair, but I need a cute outfit and my makeup never looks as good as yours."

"Makeup I can do," Wren said. "Clothes—where are you guys going?"

"Um, Parker's in Beaverton."

"Lunch or dinner?"

"Dinner."

"Is his daughter coming?"

Wren gritted her teeth. "No."

"So something flirty and sexy and that says kiss me later." Wren's eyes positively sparkled.

Dawn shook her head. "No. None of that. The opposite of that."

Wren sobered and leaned forward. "I'm confused."

So was Dawn. She sighed. "I'm...he can't possibly like me," she said. "I just need to look...more put together than I normally do." She gestured to her plain blue jeans and floral blouse. "This is a step up from what I normally wear. He always sees me in joggers and a T-shirt at the police department. Just a couple degrees better than that is fine."

Wren stood and grabbed her purse from the bottom drawer of the desk. "I think we can get you a couple of degrees up from joggers, sis. Let's go."

Dawn suppressed a groan. She'd come here for Wren's help, and she'd known shopping was a very real possibility. And if she was being honest, flirty, sexy, and something that said *kiss me later* sort of sounded like a good idea.

CHAPTER 3

McDermott paced along the end of his king-size bed, sure he should change his shirt again. "You sure it looks okay, baby?" He turned back to Taya, who colored in the spot where he normally slept. Thelma and Louise snoozed on the other side of the bed, completely unconcerned about his wardrobe choices.

"I like it, Daddy." Taya picked up a blue crayon. "It's like this color, and it's my favorite color."

He smiled at his daughter and walked over to press a kiss to her forehead. "I'll be home late. So you go to bed when Nana Reba tells you to."

"You'll come kiss me when you get in?"

"Yeah, I'll come kiss you when I get in."

Taya selected a pink crayon and colored in one of the girl's shoes on her paper. "All right, Daddy. Have fun."

He hadn't told her exactly what he was doing, or where he was going, or who he was going with. He'd said he needed to go out and that he needed to look nice when he did. As he left her in his bedroom, he couldn't help feeling like he was doing the wrong thing.

No, he told himself. Taya would be fine. They'd spent the day together, first at the horse farm, and then in the strawberry fields. She was happy the pool would open on Monday, and he'd promised to take her right when they opened.

He could go out tonight, guilt-free.

"Nana, I'm headed out. She can stay up as late as you can stand her." He flashed his grandmother a smile, hoping to get out the door without much fanfare, as he pocketed his wallet and picked up his keys.

She hurried to set her knitting aside and get to her feet. He'd almost made it to the front door before she intercepted him. "You look very nice, McDermott." Her fingers flitted along his collar, smoothing it down. "Are you nervous?"

"No, Nana. I've been out with women before." He'd tried dates with several different women over the course of the last year, but none of them held his interest. Because none of them were Dawn Fuller. She'd dominated his thoughts for a solid year, and he was nothing short of terrified that their date wouldn't go well.

"All right," Nana said like she didn't believe him. "Have fun."

He hoped he would. He shrugged into his leather jacket and headed out to his cruiser. He didn't have another car, and he suddenly realized it might be stupid to show up in his police vehicle. "You have for your other dates," he muttered to himself. "No one minded then."

Still, Dawn wasn't an average woman, McDermott knew that much. He parked, climbed the steps, and knocked on her door, his pulse kicking into a new gear with each action.

She pulled open the door, already wearing a smile. "McDermott. Hello."

He didn't have enough brain power to speak. All of his resources were devoted to drinking in the sight of her waves of blonde hair, each falling in perfect curls over both of her shoulders. She wore a pink and white dress that hugged her body and flared at her waist. White heeled sandals completed the flirty look, and she clutched a purse the color of sunshine on a summer day.

"You look nice," she said, taking a single step forward and brushing one hand along his collar. "Blue suits you."

"Thank you," he managed to say. "You look very pretty." He offered her his arm, thrilled when she looped her hand through it and they went down the stairs together. Every cell in his body blazed with electricity and heat, but he managed to ask her about her family and then her job, neither of which she talked about much.

The scent of powder and grapefruit filled his cruiser, and he realized it was a very bad idea to let her sit in his car. Now he'd have to smell her—and thus torture himself—every time he went to work.

"So talk to me about this horseback riding thing," she said.

Thankful for something to talk about, McDermott said, "Taya and I go up to the horse farm almost every Saturday morning. She likes this big, beautiful horse named Cinnamon." He smiled at his daughter's exuberance. "And there's a bunch of dogs up there she loves to play with."

"Oh, I love dogs."

"I have two golden retrievers," he said. "They're sisters. Thelma and Louise."

She giggled and crossed her legs, which only made McDermott want to stare at her for several long minutes. With great effort, he kept his eyes on the road, glad the beginning of summer meant the sun wouldn't set for another hour or so.

"Now that school's out, she'll want to go up to the farm all the time," he said. "Nana Reba will take her sometimes, but they spend a lot of time at the strawberry fields too."

"I'd like to go do the you-pick," she said, brushing her curls over her shoulder. "You can arrange that, right?"

"Any time you want," he said. "Sometimes we go up to help out before the fields open."

"Like, you volunteer? At your own family's fields?"

McDermott shrugged and turned into the Parker's parking lot. "Yeah, sure. Stay put. I'll come get the door for you." Thankfully, Dawn let him play the gentleman and hold the door for her and they made it in to the restaurant. It was busy, with lots of people involved in their own conversations. He crammed himself against the wall to wait, and Dawn pressed closer and closer to him as more patrons arrived. He finally threaded his fingers through hers and turned sideways so she could fit easier.

"Sorry," he said, though he wasn't sorry about anything that was happening at the moment.

Her hand tightened against his. Conversation was difficult in the loud lobby, but when they got to the table, he asked her if she still played the fiddle.

She stilled in her motion of spreading her napkin across her lap. "I can't believe you remember that I play the fiddle."

McDermott couldn't seem to look away from her. "You won the talent contest for Strawberry Day three years in a row. How could I forget?"

With the dim lighting in the restaurant, he wasn't quite sure if she was blushing, but it sure looked like it. "I don't play much any more."

"No? Why'd you stop?"

She shrugged one shoulder. "Got busy."

McDermott didn't think that was the reason why, but he didn't want to play cop on this date. "You like your job, don't you?"

"Oh, sure." She sipped her water as the waitress came

to take their orders. She started talking about some of the escapades that had happened during her nightly cleaning, and McDermott enjoyed himself immensely.

When he got back to her apartment, he tucked his hands into his pockets and hung back as she opened the door. "This was fun," he said, telling himself not to ask her if she'd liked the date. He didn't want to seem needy, and what if she said no?

She turned back to him wearing a gorgeous smile. "You know what? I had a great time."

"So strawberry picking? You really want to do that?"

"Sure."

"I'm working Memorial Day, and I promised Taya I'd take her to the pool that day. I don't work Tuesday."

"I work evenings," she said. "We could go in the morning." She fiddled with his collar, sending a thrill zipping through all his bones. "But not too early. I'm a late sleeper."

"You say when."

"Eleven?"

McDermott thought it would be warm by eleven, but he'd sweat through strawberry picking if he could spend time with Dawn. "Want to stop by my place and pick me up?" he asked. "It's on the way up."

"Sure." She stepped up to him and tipped onto her toes. Her lips touched his cheek and she withdrew quickly. "See you Tuesday." She moved into the apartment and turned back to close the door.

"What about church?" McDermott blurted, regretting his words only a moment later. Sitting in church with Dawn would require explanations to Taya, and she wasn't ready for that. He probably wasn't either.

Dawn blinked and he said, "Nope. Never mind." He lifted his hand and backed up a step. "Good night, Dawn." He made it down the steps and out the door into the cool evening air, a sigh hissing from his mouth once he was in the clear.

"Real smooth," he said as he climbed behind the wheel. He'd been out of the dating game for a while, though he'd gone out with a few women. Because as he'd just learned, there was a difference between going to dinner with someone he wasn't interested in and one who made his heart hammer beneath his ribs.

––––––––

MCDERMOTT SAW Dawn's blonde waves when he got to church on Sunday. She didn't sit by her family, but all alone on the left side. He wanted to talk to her, but he schooled himself into submission. He sat in his family's regular spot, his daughter between him and Nana Reba. After the sermon he barely heard as he kept trying to catch a whiff of Dawn's perfume, he let Taya run across the bridge and into Oxbow Park.

"We'll take Nana Reba back with us," his mom said, stretching up to kiss his cheek.

"Thanks, Mom."

"You'll come for lunch?"

He turned away from Dawn, who'd just exited the church. "Yeah, of course."

They moved away, and he kept his eyes on his daughter as she skipped toward the swings and squirmed into one. His feet had just hit the bridge when Dawn called his name.

He half-turned, so he could respond to her as well as keep watch over Taya. "Hey," he said as she clicked closer in her heels. They lifted her up three inches, and he liked the shiny blackness of them paired with her bright red dress.

His mouth turned dry, especially when she slipped her hand in his and walked with him across the bridge. "So it's not Tuesday," he said.

She glanced at him, confusion evident on her face. "No, it's not."

"You just seemed like you didn't want to see me again until Tuesday."

Her mouth flattened into a straight line, and McDermott kicked himself again. Was he trying to push her away?

She nodded toward Taya. "I wasn't sure about her, honestly." She paused, tugging gently on McDermott's hand to get him to stop. "What have you told her?" She faced him, her chin lifting in a move of defiance. "How will you introduce me?"

His fingers tightened on hers. "Taya is six," he said. "So no, I haven't told her much about the women I go out with."

"Oh, so there's a lot of us?"

"No," he said. "One every once in a while, and all they do is remind me that they're not you." He groaned when he realized what he'd said, and he shook his hand out of Dawn's. "Forget I said that."

CHAPTER 4

Dawn could absolutely not forget what McDermott had just said. Surprise mixed with pleasure inside her, and all she wanted to do was meet his daughter, eat lunch with him, tell him everything about her life so it would stop festering inside her.

"McDermott," she said, at a loss for what else to add. His dark eyes stormed with emotion, and she hated that he'd removed his hand from hers.

He kept his eyes on his daughter as he said, "If you want to meet her, you can. I'd call you my friend, because well, you are my friend, and I'm not sure we're to the girl-friend stage yet." He swallowed, and the word "girl-friend" prompted Dawn to do the same.

"What does it take to get to the girlfriend stage with you?" she asked.

His gaze flew back to hers, and the heat from it

infected her right down to her pinky toes. "More than holding hands and going out to dinner once."

"How much more?" she pressed. She'd lain awake last night for at least an hour, reliving the date. Everything he'd said. Every time he'd laughed. What she'd told him. How he'd reacted to it. The whole evening had been exhausting and exhilarating at the same time.

She liked McDermott. They *had* gotten along real nice, as he'd said he thought they would. They shared several things in common, and she'd woken that morning wishing it were Tuesday so she could see him again.

Then she realized she could. He went to church every week, same as her.

"Look," she said when he still hadn't defined when a woman became his girlfriend. "I like you, but I'm...."

"I already know," he said. "I told you we could go slow. You're the one who came over and started holdin' my hand again." He smiled at her, a soft, simple smile that helped her relax. "My parents are having lunch at their place today. You could come."

Meeting his daughter and his parents in one day felt like a total girlfriend move. "I—I don't think so."

"Too much, huh?"

"Maybe I can just meet Taya for now. See if she likes me at all."

"She's six," he said again. "We're not going to make our adult decisions based on how she feels." He took a step toward her, stalling again when Dawn didn't even move. "What?" he asked.

"We're not? You aren't concerned about her reaction to her father dating? Getting remarried? Any of that?" She couldn't believe she'd used the word *remarried*. What was she doing?

Stop talking, she told herself as she sucked in a breath.

"Look who's thinkin' really far down the road," McDermott said with a flirty smile. "Honestly, Dawn. I think you're making this harder than it needs to be."

Pastor Peters had said something similar, and that only added frustration to Dawn's humiliation. "All right, you're right." She stepped with him, careful to keep her hands tucked into her skirt pockets now, as she didn't want Taya to see her holding hands with McDermott.

"Want me to push you, baby?" he asked, his deep trooper voice gentle and loving for his daughter.

"Yep." Her toes skimmed the dirt, but she couldn't really get a good push herself. McDermott stood behind her and got her going so high she squealed and laughed. "Slow me down, Daddy!" she called, and he obliged. "I'm gonna jump, okay? You tell me when I can jump."

"Just a sec," he said, moving to stand in front of her now. Dawn's heart pittered and pattered at the sense of family, their love for each other. She very much wanted to feel that, but she wasn't sure of so many things.

Her family was loud, obnoxious, overbearing. She'd never had private, sincere moments like this growing up, because there were simply too many kids, too much to do, too little time.

"Wait," he said. "You've gotta let go right at the top of the swing, all right?"

Taya's face scrunched up in concentration.

"Now!" he said, and the little girl launched herself out of the swing. She landed and ran forward a few steps until McDermott swept her off her feet and back into the air. They laughed together, and he set her back on the ground. "This is my friend, Dawn." He pointed to where she stood off to the side.

"Ooh, I like her dress."

"She likes your dress," McDermott said, his eyes skating over the garment and down to her feet. "What about those shoes?"

"Mom had some shoes like that. 'Member I tried to wear them for Halloween last year?"

He chuckled and waved Dawn closer. "I remember, baby. Dang near broke your ankle."

"I clean your dad's office," Dawn said when she stood next to Taya. "He likes sour cream and onion potato chips and the German special from Gigi's. Did you know that?"

Surprise crossed the little girl's face, then she scrunched it up in disgust. "Nana Reba tells him he can't bring anything home from Gigi's." She waved her hand in front of her nose. "Says it smells sour."

Dawn laughed, grateful this tiny human wasn't shy. She'd spoken of her mother easily too, and Dawn wondered if having an instant family with McDermott and Taya wouldn't be the nightmare she'd envisioned.

"It's just sauerkraut," McDermott said, shrugging. "I like it."

"I agree with Taya. That stuff stinks." Dawn gave him a look she hoped was fun and flirty, and they started back toward the church parking lot. She waved at them and got behind the wheel of her own car, though she only lived four blocks from the church and should've walked.

Her phone chimed and McDermott had sent a message. *See? Not so bad, right?*

Dawn smiled at her screen, her thumbs already flying. *Definitely not so bad.*

You sure you don't want to come to lunch?

She looked up, feeling a bit weird to be texting him when he sat a couple of rows over in his cruiser. She wanted to spend more time with him, but the thought of meeting his parents the day after their first date didn't sit right inside her.

So she texted, *Another time. I think I'm going to go visit my great-grandfather.*

Putting the car in gear, she left him and Taya sitting in the lot. She felt better today than she had in a long, long time, and she wondered what the difference was. Maybe the fresh summer air. Maybe that she believed Pastor Peters when he said she was all right by God. Or maybe, just maybe, holding hands with a handsome man had anchored her soul and alleviated her loneliness.

An hour later, she showed up at her great-grandfather's cottage across the street from the giant house where she'd been raised. "I come bearing deviled eggs," she called as she entered the house without knocking.

"Dawn?" he called from the sunroom on the back of the house. It had been a porch for fifty years before her father had screened it in. "Is that you?"

She walked through the living room and kitchen and into the sunroom, the plate of his favorite treat in front of her. "Sure is. How are you, Gramps?" She bent down to give him a quick kiss on the cheek. "Mom said you weren't feeling up to church today."

"Oh, my old bones are tired," he said. "I'm trying to warm them up so we can get something done today."

She sat in the wicker chair on the other side of the table and put the deviled eggs between them. "What do you need to get done today?"

"Bailey needs a walk." The old English bulldog lifted her head and looked at her master, a baleful expression on her face.

"I don't think Bailey likes to walk," Dawn said with a chuckle. "I think she's just fine right there."

"Are these deviled eggs?" He reached over with shaking fingers and plucked an egg half from the plate, eating the whole thing at once. "Mm. You make the best deviled eggs."

Satisfaction flowed through Dawn. "Don't let Mom hear you say that."

"Oh, I've told her." He patted her hand and took another egg. Dawn looked past the screen to the yard beyond. Her father or brothers had obviously been here, because everything was trimmed and troweled and terrific. The breeze lifted through the centuries-old trees, and peace filled Dawn's soul.

"I went out with someone," she said, not quite sure when she'd decided to tell her great-grandfather about McDermott.

"That's nice," he said.

And that was why. He wouldn't ask a million questions. His eyes wouldn't sharpen. He wouldn't assume she'd been up to no good, or that the guy was a bum.

"It *was* nice," Dawn said, accepting that she'd had a good time with McDermott. The rest of the afternoon was equally nice, as she dozed in the sunroom, her dreams filled with the scent of McDermott's woodsy cologne and the warmth of his hand consuming hers.

When she woke, she found her great-grandfather asleep too, Bailey snoozing at his feet. A smile filled her whole soul, and she put the deviled eggs in the fridge on her way out.

———

SHE MADE it through Memorial Day without obsessively texting McDermott. It was harder than she'd thought it would be, especially as she didn't have to work that evening. After all, the banks had all been closed, and the police department cleaning went quickly as they'd mostly been out monitoring the holiday activities, the same way McDermott had been.

She half-expected him to show up in his office, as he sometimes did, but he stayed away, her phone not receiving any messages from him either.

Tuesday morning came, and she woke just after seven. She hadn't gotten up this early in years, but her nerves were hopping around her bloodstream, making sleep impossible. She ran over to the bakery to pick up an assortment of treats for their excursion to the strawberry fields, then back home to shower, primp, and waste time online until it was time to go to McDermott's.

She felt a bit odd, going to pick him up, but thankfully, he was in the front yard when she arrived. He waved to her but maintained his grip on the hose as he watered a tree that looked like it was already dead.

Gripping the steering wheel, she waited until he finished the task, took the stairs two at a time to the front door, yelled something inside, and grabbed a cowboy hat from the banister on the porch.

Dawn pulled in a long breath at the sight of him striding toward her. Tall, lean, dark, handsome, and that cowboy hat? Downright sinful. She schooled her thoughts, reminding herself that they were still in the friends category and friends didn't fantasize about removing the other's hat and sweeping their fingers through miles of dark hair moments before kissing each other.

"Mornin'," he said, bending himself into the passenger seat. "Okay, yeah. I'm not going to fit here." He reached below the seat and slid it back as far as it would go. "That's better." He turned toward her and flashed her a brilliant smile. It was a miracle this man had not been snatched up very soon after his wife had died.

For a moment, Dawn considered telling him the truth about herself. Confessing why she'd been so distracted that day, a year ago, coming home from Vernal. Revealing to him that she'd once had a life very different from the one she lived now.

Pastor Peters had assured her and reassured her that she could shed old skins. Become new through the atonement of the Savior. Repent and be whole again.

"Hey, are you okay?" he asked.

"What? Yes. Yes, I'm fine." She got the car moving out of the cul-de-sac where he lived and back to the main road that would take them up to the strawberry fields. If she wanted a real relationship with McDermott—one that went beyond friendship—she'd have to tell him eventually.

But it didn't need to be today.

CHAPTER 5

McDermott could tell Dawn was distracted, but he let her be. He'd find it annoying if she were always pushing him to talk, to say something he might not want to say. By the time they pulled into the you-pick lot at his family's fields, she seemed almost back to her fun, flirty-yet-serious self.

"So, have you done this before?" he asked as he got out of her tiny car. He didn't remember sedans being quite so small in the past.

"A long time ago." She rubbed her hands up her arms and surveyed the landscape before them. "Tell me about these fields. Your family's owned them for a long time, right?"

"As long as Brush Creek's been on the map," he said. "They're on my mother's side of the family, and my dad says he had no idea what he was getting into when he met her at the fair in Vernal." He chuckled at the story he'd heard dozens of times. "He was a banker before he met her, and well, strawberries are a far cry from currency."

He started toward the shed where they could get their cartons and crates, glad when Dawn, in all her grapefruit and powder glory, stepped to his side. She wore sneakers—sensible for their activity that morning—and a pair of cutoffs that left him with such a great view of her legs. She wore a blue T-shirt with black ribbing along the sleeves and collar, with a big black heart on the front of it.

"It probably helped, didn't it?" she asked. "His knowledge of money and finances and stuff."

"A little, I guess." McDermott stepped right up to the booth to find Kassidy there. He'd gone out with her once, almost a year ago. There'd been no spark, and he'd thought he'd done a decent job of keeping things professional and relatively normal between them.

"Hey," she said, leaning on the small shelf that separated her from the customers. "What are you doin' here?"

"We want to pick our own berries," he said. "The best ones, Kass. Don't put us in any of those puny rows, all right?"

She giggled and tossed her hair over her shoulder. Dawn stepped to his side and took his hand in hers. He wasn't sure why, but the gesture surprised him, and he tilted his head to look at her. "How many do you want?"

"I think half a flat," she said, never taking her eyes off Kassidy.

"Same for me," he said. "We can share one," he added as Kass bent to get the containers and boxes they needed. "We'll be on the same row."

She set one flat and twelve pint baskets on the shelf, her smile gone. "Row H."

"That's a good one?"

She gave him a saucy smirk. "If you don't like it, pick a row, McDermott. You own the place."

Confusion raced through him, but he picked up the box and headed to the right, behind the shed. Technically, he didn't own the place. He'd pay for his fruit just like everyone else who came to pick their own berries.

"She likes you," Dawn singsonged once they were several rows away from the shed.

"What?"

"What? You didn't notice how all flirty and hair-tossy she was? Please." Dawn laughed, the sound of it making the air taste better, the sky bluer, his soul lighter.

"Oh, so that's why you stepped right up and held my hand." He watched her, the pieces clicking into place at the guilty look on her face. "I get it now. You were jealous."

"So what if I was?" She sniffed as if she had every right to be jealous. He shook his head and chuckled, wondering why she'd turned him down for a solid year if she was going to get all jealous after only going out together once.

She was an enigma, a puzzle he hadn't quite figured out yet. She didn't seem like the type to play games, and she'd admitted she was scared of his previous marriage and that he had a child.

But he couldn't change those things about his past. He didn't want to. Every experience he'd had had shaped him into who he was today. And if she didn't like that, he didn't know what else to do.

"So I just pluck them off the vines?" she asked, staring down into the bushes.

He laid out the green plastic baskets. "Pretty much. It's not rocket science."

She nudged him with her elbow and said, "Don't make fun of me. I'd like to see you clean a bank in under an hour."

Laughter burst from his mouth. "I guess we all have different skill sets." He picked three strawberries from the bush and set them in the basket. They moved down the row together, the conversation easy, light, revolving around things that didn't really matter.

And while McDermott had never really enjoyed the bend-and-stand, stand-and-bend nature of picking strawberries, he enjoyed his time with Dawn immensely. He hoped Taya wouldn't come between them. Prayed for guidance about what to say, what to do, how to act when it came to Dawn.

In the end, all he needed to do was be himself. That seemed like enough for Dawn, and as they paid for their strawberries and held hands on the way back to town,

McDermott had never been happier that he'd listened to Walker and Tess and tried a different tactic with Dawn.

He'd asked her out in a different way this time, and when she'd turned him down, he'd called. Refused to give up. Been honest. When Walker had suggested it, McDermott had almost laughed in his face.

Gotta do something different to get something different, Tess had said. And it had worked.

"So, when's your next day off?" Dawn had delivered him right back to his house, but he wasn't ready to part ways with her yet.

Do it anyway, he told himself. He didn't want to come on too strong. He'd told her he wasn't in a hurry, and though she'd seemed to enjoy herself whenever they were together, he knew something lurked just beneath her pristine surface. He wanted to crack that ice, dive into her life, and find out everything about her.

"Saturday," he said. "Horse farm? Horseback riding?"

"You take Taya with you, right?"

"Yep."

She focused out the windshield, clearly in a battle with herself. He was just about to say, "It's fine. We'll get together in the evening," when she said. "Yeah, sure. The three of us." She faced him, a smile as glorious as the sunrise lighting her face. "Sounds fun."

"Do you own any boots?" he asked. "Or a hat?"

"I can get some."

He nodded, returning her smile. "You probably should. Walker'll make you wear some of his boots if you don't have any. He's real particular about horseback riding safety."

Quickly, before he could overthink anything, he reached over and cradled her face in his palm. He pressed a kiss to her temple, glad when she leaned into his touch. And was that a sigh?

"See you Saturday." He forced himself out of the car and all the way up the sidewalk to the front porch before he turned around. She hadn't moved, and her expression was still a bit dazed. Glad to know the attraction between them wasn't one-sided, he waved and disappeared into the house, where he flopped onto the couch with a big sigh leaking from his mouth.

"That good, huh?" Nana Reba said, peering through the cutout the connected the kitchen to the living room. "She must be something special to make a man like you go all soft."

McDermott couldn't stop smiling, the only confirmation he was willing to give at the moment. Truth was, he'd been crushing hard on Dawn ever since he'd pulled her from her wrecked car. The fact that she seemed to finally be reciprocating those feelings had his heart tap-dancing as if for the first time.

It's not the first time, he thought, and his smile slipped. He missed Amelia with a fierceness he'd never understand. Some days he didn't think about her at all.

And some days, she crept into his thoughts as easily as if she were still alive and he'd just kissed her good-bye that morning.

"Nana Reba?" He got up and went into the kitchen, where she kneaded dough for her famous honey wheat bread. "I'm not being disloyal to Amelia, am I?"

"Oh, honey," she said in her raspy voice. "Of course not."

He nodded, but his stomach felt a little knotted when it had been fine before. "Where's Taya?"

"Next door with Rosie. She just barely went over after lunch."

"I'll take Thelma and Louise down to the river." The dogs loved to swim, and though they had more hair than McDermott knew how to take care of, the sun was shining hot today, and they could lay in the backyard until they dried. And walking and watching dogs swim didn't require much mental effort on his part, leaving him plenty of time to plan his next date with Dawn. Think about Dawn. Daydream about kissing Dawn.

By the time he got home, all remnants of his earlier feelings of disloyalty had completely disappeared. McDermott didn't know if he should be glad or sad about that, but he couldn't change the past.

All he could do was look forward to a hopefully brighter, better future.

————

THE MONTH of June melted into July, with McDermott seeing Dawn a couple of times each week. They went to dinner sometimes, lunch once, and up to the horse farm to ride horses once. Dawn hadn't seemed particularly keen on that, but McDermott had a hard time deciphering what she liked and what she didn't.

She kept saying yes when he asked her to do something with him, and she even suggested some of their activities. He was being patient with her, and he really enjoyed her company, holding her hand, and listening to her talk about her life, her family, and her hopes.

He drove the highway between Brush Creek and Vernal, went out to Dinosaur National Park every week, and helped with anything the police department in town needed. His job wasn't anything too taxing, especially since he mainly handed out speeding tickets and kept the peace by his very presence.

One evening, as he drove north from Vernal when his radio crackled. "Trooper Boyd, come in."

He lifted the receiver and said, "Go for Boyd."

"A 10-50 was just reported six miles south of Beaverton, with PI. 10-52 en route, and be advised, it may be a 10-55. ETA?"

Six miles south of Beaverton? McDermott pushed down the button and said, "ETA ten minutes." He flipped on his lights and siren, pressing on the accelerator to ensure he arrived in ten minutes.

"10-4," the dispatcher said. "Bus coming from Brush Creek."

McDermott's heartbeat increased with every mile that flew beneath his tires. He saw the accident up ahead, and he grabbed the radio receiver. "On-site. Looks like a 10-54." Livestock—in this case, cows—on the road.

He eased to a stop behind the vehicle with smoke lifting from the hood. He couldn't see a human being anywhere, not even in the car, and if the driver really was intoxicated, they could be anywhere.

With anything.

McDermott spoke to the radio again. "10-23, dispatch. There's no one here. Getting out to look around."

"10-4," the female dispatcher said. "Camera is on and transmitting."

McDermott flipped the switch that would send all transmissions to the receiver he wore on his shoulder, and the last syllable of her sentence sounded there. He got out of the car slowly, standing behind the open door to scan the empty highway with this smoking car.

It had obviously hit one of the cows still crossing the highway without a care in the world. How far could someone have gotten in ten minutes? Especially if they were intoxicated?

"Hello?" McDermott called, keeping one hand on his weapon. He let his other hand hang loose as he approached the car and peered in the backseat. Empty. The driver's door was open, indicating someone had been here at some point. The blood on the front fender confirmed everything he'd suspected.

He pushed the button on his shoulder. "10-20, mile marker seventy-two. I've got a vehicle here, obviously hit a cow. No human presence. Driver's door open."

"So a 10-57?"

"A hit and run with a cow," he said. A siren sounded behind him, and he glanced over his shoulder, the red lights adding to the colors of the wilderness.

The grass down the road rustled, and McDermott stalled, trying to listen. But with the siren, he wouldn't be able to hear. He stepped cautiously that way, his mind circling Taya and begging the Lord to keep him safe if he encountered an intoxicated driver.

After several steps, he heard a distinct moan, and he waved at the ambulance to slow and stop, which they did. He pointed to the left side of the road, the grass there definitely being disturbed by something.

"Nothing back here," he called to Ed Moon, the paramedic who got out on the passenger side. Max Robinson joined him, and McDermott added, "I think he may be down there."

They hung behind him as he inched closer to the side of the road and looked down into the ditch. A man lay there, his eyes closed as if he were asleep.

"Hey," McDermott barked, causing the man to open his eyes. "State Trooper McDermott Boyd. Are you okay?"

He groaned, and his glazed eyes rolled back in his head.

"I've got two paramedics here," McDermott said. "Is

it safe to come down there? You have any weapons, knives, guns, anything like that?"

Another moan.

"I think he's pretty out of it," McDermott said. "Let me check 'im first." He went down the incline, dislodging dirt and gravel as he kept his boots from sliding. "Hey," he said again. This time, the man didn't stir at all.

"Blood on his face," he called. "He's unconscious." He patted him down, checking for sharp objects or anything that would injure the paramedics as they administered to him. "He's clear."

Ed and Max came down, carrying their heavy bags, and got to work. McDermott called in their arrival and the discovery of the man. "Did he give a name?" he asked dispatch.

"Negative."

McDermott watched as the paramedics lifted him onto a board and brought him up to the bus.

"Cleaning up," he radioed to dispatch. "I've got a 10-51."

"10-4 on 10-51."

McDermott went back to his cruiser as the ambulance turned around and went back to Brush Creek. He wished he was on his way too. He texted Nana Reba that he'd encountered a snag that would keep him for another hour and got a message back without a single capital letter or punctuation mark.

He smiled at his grandmother's stunted use of technology and settled into to direct traffic around the wreck and wait for the tow truck to get the car out of the way.

His phone chimed and he glanced at it since there weren't any cars on the road at the moment.

Dawn's name made his heart stutter-step in his chest.

Nana Reba said you're going to be late. Everything okay?

He wasn't sure why Nana had let Dawn know about his tardiness. They weren't supposed to be getting together tonight.

Fine, he tapped out. A car approached and he pocketed his phone so he could do his job. He waved them around the wreckage, glad when a tow truck with Mick's red and blue logo showed up and Mick himself got out.

"McDermott," he said. "We've really gotta stop meeting out here."

McDermott smiled and said, "You should come over for dinner after this."

"Yeah? What did Nana Reba make?"

"I don't know; haven't been home yet, but I'm sure it'll be something you like." Mick was a single dad too, but his wife was still alive and remarried. They lived out in Nielson's Grove, north and west of Brush Creek.

Mick had a daughter a couple of years older than Taya, and he only saw her on the weekends. Since McDermott often had to take care of traffic accidents, he'd become good friends with Mick over the years.

He got the car hooked up and ready to roll in record

time, and McDermott followed the tow truck through Beaverton and into Brush Creek. When he pulled around the corner and entered the cul-de-sac where he lived, he found Dawn's sedan parked in front of the house.

It was then that he realized he'd never responded to her text.

Chapter 6

Dawn was just going to wait in her car. Just to make sure McDermott made it home safely. She wasn't even sure why she was so worried. But Reba Sholes had never texted her before—Dawn wasn't even sure how the older woman had gotten her number.

But she also peered through the curtains to check on the neighborhood, and Dawn had been sitting in front of the house for three minutes before Reba came out and insisted she come wait inside the house.

So she sat on the couch when McDermott pushed through the door that led into the kitchen. The steady sound of his boots on the tile brought relief to her, and the low cadence of his voice made her shiver.

She'd been toying with the idea of telling him about the reinvention of herself over the past year. She knew she'd have to tell him what she was doing in Vernal that day she'd gone off the road, and she wasn't sure how he'd react.

But she wanted him to know, because he'd shared important things with her. Personal, intimate things about how he missed his wife, how he prayed before he left for work each day and thanked God each evening when he returned safely. His devotion and love for his daughter was evident in everything he said, everything he did.

Dawn marveled every time he texted her, or asked her out, or held her hand that he really seemed to like her.

He appeared in the doorway that led into the kitchen, still wearing his trooper hat with the flat brim and all his accessories around his waist. He was single-handedly the sexiest man she'd ever laid eyes on, and she leapt to her feet.

"You're okay."

"Sorry I didn't respond. I was directing traffic around this accident." He entered the living room but leaned against the corner of the wall that led down the hall to the bedrooms. "What are you doin' here?"

"Oh, uh, nothing."

He didn't believe her, if the mischievous glint in his eye said anything. And it did. A lot. "Worried about me?"

So what if she was? He was a state trooper, for crying out loud. His wife had been killed on the job. "Maybe," Dawn said.

Something heated passed between them, and McDermott took off his trooper hat and went over to the hat rack by the front door to hang it up. "Want to go for a walk?"

"It's got to be a hundred degrees outside," she said.

"The sun's on the way down."

She scoffed. "It doesn't get dark until almost ten, McDermott. Nice try."

His fingers brushed hers. A feathered touch. Light. There, then gone. She wanted him to grab ahold of her hand and claim her as his. She wasn't sure when her thoughts had started derailing, but it was probably about the time she'd decided to tell him the truth about her past.

"Are we still on for the fireworks on Friday?"

"You're not working them?"

"I'll wear my uniform, yes," he said. "But I'm not officially on duty."

"It'll just look like you are."

"Right," he said. "You'd be surprised how well that keeps the peace."

The thought of curling up next to him in the park with hundreds of other people actually appealed to Dawn. She couldn't believe it, and that alone was a testimony of how far she'd come since her own accident last year.

"Yeah, we're still good for that."

"Taya and Nana Reba are comin' too." He lifted his hand and ran his fingertips along her neck.

Dawn shivered and let her eyes fall closed. His touch was magical, and it sent her heartbeat into a tizzy. "Let's go for a walk," she blurted, stepping around him and heading for the front door.

He called into his grandmother and then joined her on the porch. "We could drive," he said. "Your car has air conditioning."

"Drive where?" she asked.

"Just drive," he said.

Dawn wasn't sure she could be in charge of a vehicle and talk to McDermott the way she wanted to. "Will you drive?" She held out her keys.

He narrowed his eyes for just a moment and then took the keys. "Sure." Ever the gentleman, he opened the door for her, and she ran her hands along her shorts, already sweating. Once he got in and got the car started, the air cooled quickly.

He drove north, toward the strawberry fields and parked in the shade of the huge trees that grew along the river up here. A riverwalk ran along them, and it went all the way down into town, to Oxbow Park. But he made no move to get out of the car.

"It was just an accident tonight," he said. "A vehicle meets livestock accident. One car. Guy was drunk."

"Did you see it?"

"No. Dispatch called me to it."

"Is the guy all right?"

"Ed and Max brought him to the hospital here." He shrugged. "I can check on him tomorrow." He stared out the windshield, and she wondered what he was seeing in his mind.

"Why did you ask me out so much?" she asked, twisting toward him and tucking her leg under her body.

He swung his attention to her. "You're Dawn Fuller."

She scoffed for the second time that night. "That means nothing."

He tucked a curl behind her ear and it took everything she had not to lean into him. "You're beautiful. I'm attracted to you."

"And?" Because if there was one thing Dawn knew, attraction only went so far.

"I like spending time with you. I was right, you know. We get along real nice." He leaned his head back against the headrest and gazed at her with a melty, soft look in his eyes. She'd seen him do such a thing several times before, and it made her feel...loved.

"But you didn't know that before," she said. "And you asked me out relentlessly for twelve months."

He smiled, not quite the reaction she'd been expecting. "You were kind to me when Amelia died," he whispered. "You brought sandwiches and you didn't ask me how I was doing."

Dawn started to relive the memory as he continued. "You cried, and your voice choked when you said 'I'm so sorry, McDermott. I can't bring her back, but I would if I could.' And you sort of flung the plate of sandwiches on the counter, and you hugged my mom and dad, and you even had a toy for Taya."

Emotions teemed just below Dawn's skin. She looked

away, out through her passenger window. "That was a long time ago, McDermott."

"I remember it like it was yesterday." He brushed his fingers along her knee, finally settling them in hers. "I was out of it for a while after the funeral. Probably a year or so. That's what my mom says, at least. I didn't want to date anyone for another year. And then I started thinking about it. I went out with a few women. You were always right at the top of my list, but it was like you were unreachable. Until the accident. After that, I knew I wanted you even though I kept trying to find someone else."

"I probably only made the sandwiches so I would have something to eat too," she said, his words reverberating around inside her mind, filling her ears, swelling in her soul. *I wanted you.*

You were always right at the top of my list.

He chuckled. "Right. Because you don't like cooking much."

She nodded, still unable to look at him though she gripped his fingers with all the strength she had.

"I have to tell you something," she said. "It's about the accident."

"All right."

She glanced at him quickly, but it proved to be too difficult. He was so kind, so handsome, so faithful. Could he even fathom her carelessness?

"I can't do it here," she said, releasing his hand and getting out of the car. Though it was hot, the shade made the air cool enough to breathe, and Dawn didn't feel so trapped.

He joined her and they wandered down the riverwalk toward his parents' strawberry fields. The ripe scent of the berries floated on the air, and the sound of the river rushed alongside them.

"I was in Vernal that day to get a pregnancy test," she said, going straight for the bullseye. McDermott said nothing but gathered her hand in his again. "See, for a while there, I lived up to my reputation as the Fuller wild child. I had a lot of boyfriends, and I made a lot of mistakes, and that was the biggest one."

Several steps were taken before he asked, "Were you pregnant?"

She shook her head, the emotion and relief from that day still as fresh as ever. "No, the test was negative. I was so happy about that, I was crying. Everything was all shook up, and remember how I told you I like to drive too fast? Well, with all of that combined, I didn't even see the deer until it was too late."

He released her hand and put his arm around her waist, drawing her closer to him. Pausing, he took her into his arms. "That must've just been the cherry on top of a terrible day."

Feeling safe and secure in his arms, she wound her arms around him too and pressed her cheek over his heartbeat. "I said no to you for a long time," she said. "I'm sorry about that, but you have to understand I wasn't in a place to be dating. I've been working with

Pastor Peters to get back on the right track, and I think I'm getting close."

"You're already there, Dawn." He inched back and looked down at her. "You're one of the nicest, kindest, most sincere people I've ever met. You help others. You have nothing to be ashamed of."

Her eyes brimmed with tears. "But you don't know—"

"And I don't need to," he said. "I can see it, Dawn. You shine when I look at you. Like an angel from heaven."

She snorted and hiccupped all at the same time. "Is that a pick-up line?"

He laughed, the sound flying up into the tree branches, which held it and echoed it back to them. "No, sweetheart. It's how I feel about you."

Dawn felt like she'd just gotten off the tallest, wildest roller coaster in the world. She'd told him, and he hadn't judged her. Hadn't asked her who she'd been sleeping with. Didn't even seem to care that she wasn't as inexperienced as she should've been. How could he be so patient with her? So forgiving of ugly things?

She managed to say, "I sure do like you, McDermott, even if you don't shine when I look at you." She gazed up at him, her eyes traveling from his to his mouth. She licked her lips in anticipation of kissing him out here where it smelled like strawberries and sunshine.

He leaned down and she tipped up on her toes, and the first touch of his lips to hers made stars burst behind her closed eyes. So maybe there *was* a shininess to him she hadn't seen until now.

He kissed her gently, increasing to a more firm, demanding stroke, the same way he did with everything. He pulled back much sooner than she would've liked and whispered, "This is okay? It's not too soon?"

Dawn simply responded by kissing him again.

Chapter 7

McDermott had been dreaming—while awake and asleep—about kissing Dawn for a solid six months. The real event was twice as intoxicating as anything his mind had been able to come up with.

She tasted like mint and sugar, and he simply could not get enough of her. He felt himself falling at a rapid pace now, and he forced himself to breathe in deep through his nose and pull away. A gust of wind kicked up at the same time Dawn giggled and laid her head over his heartbeat again.

A squirrel of embarrassment ran through him at how quickly his pulse pounded—surely she'd hear it. He decided he didn't care. Holding her in his arms, close to his heart, was right where he wanted her, and he enjoyed the moments while he could.

"We should get back," he finally said. "I told Nana Reba we wouldn't be gone long, and I was already late."

She practically shot out of his embrace. "Of course. Yeah." She smoothed her hair down like it had gotten rumpled during their kiss and someone would know.

"Plans tonight?" he asked.

"It's Wednesday," she said. "I was thinking of going to the family dinner."

"Oh, right. Those are on Wednesdays." He wondered if she'd ever invite him to one, but he didn't ask. Just because she'd kissed him didn't mean she was ready to introduce him to the whole family or talk about diamond rings or where they'd live once they were married.

McDermott's thoughts spun wildly as he drove back to his place. He couldn't believe he'd catapulted himself to marriage already. He'd just barely kissed Dawn, and she'd just told him a heavy truth.

He honestly didn't care much about her past—only about what kind of person she was now. He'd learned some lessons like that growing up, and he'd had to figure out how to let go of the past in order to move forward when Amelia died.

After parking behind his cruiser, he killed the engine to go inside, but Dawn said, "I'm not going to stay, if that's okay."

"Oh, sure." He fired up the engine again and left it running for her while he climbed out. She met him near the corner of the hood and placed one hand on his chest.

"Thank you, McDermott."

"For what?" He liked her so much, from those perfectly sky-blue eyes to her honeyed hair to her charming spirit.

"For being you." She smiled up at him, and while McDermott had wondered if he would ever be worthy enough for Dawn Fuller, he felt like he was. In that single moment, with her looking at him with that edge of desire in her eyes, he was good enough for her.

"See you Friday?" she asked.

If he could stand not driving over to the police department tonight and pressing her into the filing cabinets in his office as he kissed her, then definitely he'd see her Friday. "Sure," he said, his voice only mildly strained, thankfully.

She tipped up on her toes again, kissing him one final time before ducking into her car and backing out of the driveway. McDermott watched her go, sure he'd just imagined the last hour of his life.

But when he entered the kitchen and Nana Reba took one look at him and asked, "What's wrong with you, McDermott? You're flushed," he knew it had been no dream.

———

He spent the next day at his desk, catching up on paperwork from June. He generally loathed days spent inside, but with the heat reaching record temperatures already, he decided it wasn't that big of a deal.

Near lunchtime, he texted Dawn to see if she wanted to meet him at Ruby's Roost for a quick sandwich, but two seconds later, her brother walked in and sat in the only chair across from McDermott's desk.

"Kyler." McDermott laughed and stood up to give his old friend a quick embrace. "What brings you by?"

Kyler had grown his hair out over the past couple of years and it nearly reached his shoulders now. He grinned at McDermott and said, "So I guess my sister finally said yes to one of your invites."

McDermott wished he wore his trooper hat so he could duck his head and hide the emotions streaming through his whole body—and surely onto his face too. "She did."

"How long ago?"

"Oh, I don't know. Five or six weeks."

"Five or six weeks?" Kyler's words indicated he was upset, but his expression said he wasn't. "And I have to hear about it at the family dinner?"

The paperwork forgotten, McDermott leaned forward. "What did she say?"

"Oh, she was whispering to Wren and Berlin about something, and I happened to overhear."

"And what did you overhear?"

"She said she was dating someone and it had suddenly gotten serious."

McDermott's face exploded into a grin.

"So what does that mean?" Kyler asked.

"How did you know it was me?"

"Well, since I know you're interested in her, I sat right down and butted into their conversation." His blue eyes were more the color of dark wash blue jeans, and they sparkled like he knew exactly what McDermott had done at the strawberry fields last night.

"She said it was you."

"It's me," McDermott said, leaning back. "And you're okay with that, right? I mean, I know she's your sister, but it's not like we're sixteen."

"Which would be totally weird," Kyler said. "Because if you were sixteen, she'd be ten."

McDermott shook his head. "You know what I mean."

"I don't think anyone has a problem with it," Kyler said.

"Did she say anything else?" He felt like a teenager, needing his best friend to spy on the girl he liked. "Never mind. I'm an adult."

But Kyler had heard something, and he cocked his head. "What are you worried about?"

McDermott didn't want to say. But he couldn't get his voice to say "Nothing," either.

"Come on," Kyler said. "Let's go get that grilled cheese you like at Ruby's." He stood, and since McDermott hadn't heard from Dawn and he did need to eat, he went with Kyler.

They walked across the street and through the park to Ruby's, where there was hardly a table to be found. With two seats available at the counter, they ordered their meals, and Kyler said, "It's Taya, right?"

"It's Taya," McDermott said.

"She was so young when Amelia died," Kyler said. "I think she'll be okay with Dawn."

McDermott looked at Kyler as confusion raced through him. "I'm not worried about how Taya will react to Dawn. I'm worried about Dawn being ready to handle Taya."

Kyler nearly spit out his soda, and when he looked at McDermott, the surprise was evident in his wide eyes. "You don't think Dawn will be a good mom?"

"I'm sure she would be," McDermott said. "If she wanted to be a mom at all." His mood darkened, even when his cheesy, Texas-toast sandwich was placed in front of him with a mountain of French fries on the side.

"She wants to go slow," McDermott said. "So maybe it won't last." In his mind, though, he saw him and Dawn welcoming more children into their family for years to come. If she ever found that out, their relationship would be in trouble. He'd promised her slow, and he was going to honor that.

"She seemed pretty committed," Kyler said. "She was quizzing Wren about how she knew she was ready to be a mom."

McDermott bit into his sandwich so he wouldn't

have to talk. He didn't want to know what Dawn had been talking about with her sisters. She'd told him she hadn't been to the family party in several months, but Kyler didn't act like it was abnormal for her to show up last night.

Thankfully, Kyler seemed to sense that McDermott didn't want to talk about his love life anymore. They ate in silence, and then he threw a twenty dollar bill on the counter. "On me, bro."

"Thanks, *bro*," McDermott said with a laugh.

"Yeah, I'm thinking of cutting the hair."

"I would agree with that decision." McDermott didn't really care what Kyler did with his hair, other than that it was a symbol that he hadn't gotten over Katie yet. And it had been years since his almost-fiancée had skipped town with nothing more than a note on his front door.

"Catch you later," Kyler said, once they'd made it back to the police station.

Friday night finally came, and McDermott knelt in front of Taya to help her with her sandals. "So we're meetin' Miss Dawn there," he said, slipping the strap through the buckle. He looked up at his daughter. "I'm dating her, Tay. She's my girlfriend." He watched her for any reaction, but Taya just blinked at him. "Do you know what that means?"

"Like, you like her, and she likes you, and you hold hands." She spoke in her innocent, high-pitched voice, and McDermott smiled.

"Right. We'll probably hold hands tonight."

"And you kiss her." Taya made a face, then she stared right into his eyes. "Daddy, do you kiss her?"

Nana Reba appeared in the doorway, and McDermott's face heated. He focused on Taya's other shoe as he said, "Yeah, Tay. I kiss her sometimes."

"Gross," Taya said.

"You like Miss Dawn, right?" he asked, glancing at his grandmother. She wore a knowing smile on her face, with only love streaming from her expression.

"I like her, yeah," Taya said.

McDermott sat back on his heels. "All right then. Let's go see some fireworks."

"You said we could get a corndog first."

"It won't be dark for hours," he said. "We have plenty of time for all kinds of things."

"For the Ferris wheel?" Taya skipped to the front door, her red, white, and blue dress billowing as she went.

He groaned. "I hate the Ferris wheel."

Taya didn't seem to hear him at all as she opened the door and left. He sighed and turned back to Nana. "Don't say anything," he said as he pocketed his wallet and keys.

"So this one's serious."

McDermott grinned at her and swept a kiss across her aged cheek. "Super serious, Nana. I like her."

"You deserve a second chance, honey."

"It's early still," he said. "See you later."

He grabbed his trooper hat as he followed his daughter out the front door, hoping that tonight would be a Fourth of July worth remembering.

Chapter 8

Dawn wasn't sure where she parked or how she made it up to the third floor in the hospital. All she knew was she now stood at the counter with a sign that said Maternity behind it. "Wren Fuller?" She shook her head and took a deep breath. "Curtis. Wren Curtis."

The nurse looked down at a planner in front of her. "Room 3491."

Dawn palmed her way through the plastic door and turned right, according to the sign. "3491, 3491," she muttered. Of course it had to be the room in the very corner.

She paused outside the door and calmed herself again. The whole family had probably crammed themselves in this tiny room, and no one would notice her anyway. She knocked as she entered, and she found the room dark except for the sliver of light from the window and the flashing light from the television in the corner.

"Hey," Tate said as he rose from the chair in the corner. He bounced their newborn as he bent toward his wife. "Wren, Dawn's here."

Wren, lying in the bed, opened her eyes, a smile coming almost immediately. "Hey."

Dawn crossed the small room, surprised no one else was here. "How are you?" she asked her sister. She looked terrible, even in the dim light, with dark circles under her eyes and a weariness in her expression that only hours of sleep could erase.

"Good." She returned Dawn's quick squeeze. "Tate's got the baby."

He came around the end of the bed to let Dawn see the infant. "You want to meet one of your aunts? This is Aunt Dawn." He cooed at the baby in a very un-police-like fashion, and Dawn marveled at the change in the tough military man who'd scared her the first time she'd met him.

"What did you name her?" Dawn asked.

"Henrietta, after Tate's mom," Wren said. "We're going to call her Etta."

"Etta." Dawn said the name with reverence, and she swept her fingers across the baby's bald head. "No hair." She grinned at Wren and then Tate.

"You want to hold her?" Tate offered the baby to her, and Dawn balked completely.

She backed up a step. "Uh, no, I'm good."

Tate looked at her with questions in his eyes, but Wren saved her by saying, "I'll take her, sweetheart." She pushed herself higher in bed and extended her arms for her daughter.

Dawn's heart felt like someone had ripped it from her body and thrown it in a blender. Somehow it kept beating, but it was irregular and so, so loud. Wren handled the baby with ease, like she'd had years of practice, and Etta gave a little groan that made her and Tate grin like they'd just achieved world peace, right there in a hospital room in Brush Creek.

She saw the love and adoration for their daughter, felt it permeate the whole room. Dawn had spent several evenings with McDermott and Taya, and while she liked the little girl, it was nowhere near the level of love both Tate and Wren exuded.

Tears gathered in her eyes at the realization. They'd had fun at the fireworks. They'd gone horseback riding again, and the more Dawn did it, the more she liked it. She'd gone with them when they'd taken their dogs to the park.

The three of them got along great. Dawn appreciated that McDermott didn't push her to go faster, but he seemed content with the speed at which they were getting to know one another. Maybe he was being cautious because he'd been down this path before. Or maybe he could sense her hesitancy.

No matter what, standing in that hospital room, she knew she was nowhere ready to be a mother. Which was a real problem, because if she took things much farther with McDermott, she'd be a mom on Day One. At least Wren and Tate had been married for a couple of years already. Dawn wouldn't get a buffer at all.

She started for the door, not even stopping when Wren said, "You're going?"

Out in the hall, she pressed her back into the wall and tried to breathe. *Calm down*, she told herself. *You're not his wife.*

But somewhere in the back of her mind, the word *yet* screamed at her, only fueling her panic. She needed to get out of this hospital, especially this ward, where there were so many new moms and their babies.

WHEN HER PHONE RANG LATER, she sat on a bench in the park, looking at the lake. She had no idea how she'd gotten there, or what time it was, or how long she'd been there.

The call was from McDermott, and she considered ignoring it. It wouldn't be the first time she'd missed one of his calls. She had a life too. But something told her to answer, and she'd learned to listen to those impressions.

"Hello?" she answered as if she didn't know who was on the other end of the line.

"Hey," he said, his voice different than ever before. "Where are you?"

She looked around. "Oxbow Park."

"I need help," he said. "Nana Reba just called in a panic, and I couldn't quite get the whole story out of her. Something's wrong with Taya, and I need you to go over there and see what's going on."

She'd never heard him say so much, so quickly.

"Sure," she said, standing.

"Great. I'm stuck in Vernal, and I can't get there."

"I'll take care of it." She hung up and crossed the street to find her car in the hospital parking lot, which took several long minutes. When she pulled up to McDermott's house, Nana Reba came flying out the front door.

"Thank goodness you're here. I think she broke her leg."

Dawn froze to the sidewalk, sure Nana Reba was wrong. "Broke her leg?"

"Come on, come on!" Nana Reba waved at her frantically.

"Did you call the ambulance?" Dawn followed her inside, where McDermott's white-haired daughter lay on the couch, seemingly asleep. "Is she unconscious?"

"She was fine." Nana Reba rushed around the couch and knelt in front of Taya. Dawn thought she'd be calling the ambulance for both of them if Nana Reba didn't slow down. And what would she tell McDermott then?

She pulled out her phone and dialed 9-1-1. She watched Taya's chest rise and fall as the operator said, "State your emergency."

"I'm with Taya Boyd," she said, her voice surprisingly

even. "She's six years old, and she's unconscious. Her great-grandmother thinks she may have a broken leg. We need an ambulance." Dawn didn't trust herself to carry the little girl to the car, and she knew McDermott could afford the transportation fee.

"Taya." Nana Reba had tears streaming down her face, and Dawn went around the couch to comfort her too.

"An ambulance is on the way. Tell me what happened."

"She was playing with the dogs in the backyard, and I heard a scream." The older woman sniffled, and Dawn patted her shoulder. "I went to see what was wrong, and she couldn't walk. Thelma wouldn't leave her side."

Even now, the golden retriever sat right next to Taya's head.

"Did she say what happened?"

"She couldn't stop crying. I call-called McDermott, but—"

"He called me," Dawn said. "He's in Vernal today, Nana." She didn't know how to fill the silence between them, and only Nana Reba's soft crying provided the background.

"Emergency services," a man called, and Dawn rushed to open the screen door for him.

"Ed, come in." She pointed to the couch. "We think she broke her leg. Nana Reba said she was playing in the backyard when she screamed. She was crying and she couldn't get her to calm down. McDermott called me." She wrung her hands, unsure of what to do for anyone.

Ed and his partner Max checked out Taya, and then turned their attention to Nana Reba. In the end, everyone except Dawn was loaded into the ambulance and taken to the hospital.

So she found herself back at the one place that had triggered her panic for the second time that day. She sat in the emergency waiting room, and Nana Reba joined her only a few minutes later.

"I'm okay," she said. "My blood pressure was elevated for a few minutes."

Dawn didn't know what to do, so she just reached over and took the elderly woman's hand in hers.

"Have you called McDermott?" she asked.

Dawn startled. She'd been so far inside her head she hadn't thought to keep those lines of communication open. "No. I'll text him now." She found texting him much easier when he was working, as he could rarely answer his phone on the job.

She let him know they were at the hospital, waiting to find out the news on Taya. Might be a broken leg, she tapped out before sending the message. I thought for a minute there, Nana Reba would go down too. They checked her out, and she's okay now that she's calmed down. We're in the waiting room together.

She gripped her phone, her frustration and worries swirling together into an intolerable tornado of emotions. She couldn't handle stress like this. And she needed to go to work in less than an hour.

She'd known she wasn't ready to be a mother last year, and not that much had changed in the last twelve months—at least not in that regard. She felt miles away from where she'd been when she'd woken up in McDermott's spare bedroom, but in much different ways than he and Taya needed at the moment.

I'm on my way. McDermott's message made relief run through Dawn. He would come. He would take care of things. He knew what to do and what to say, and she found that as attractive as it was upsetting.

He deserved someone so much better than her. Someone with at least equal skills and equal emotional strength to offer. Dawn simply couldn't give him—or his daughter—what he needed.

Her feet begged her to get up and leave. Nana Reba was here. If the doctor came out with news of Taya, she had a family member to receive it. Dawn wasn't needed.

You're not needed anywhere.

The voice that had tormented her for so many years was suddenly so loud in her head. She'd managed to silence it as she worked to get herself back into God's good graces. Why was it screaming at her again?

She got to her feet and looked toward the emergency exit.

"Where are you going?" Nana Reba asked.

"McDermott's on his way." Dawn couldn't face him. "I have to get to work."

"Oh, all right, dear. I'll tell him."

With Nana's blessing, Dawn headed for the exit. She'd stepped into the sunshine and taken two strides when she slammed into a brick wall of a man. She yelped, trying to find something to grab onto so she wouldn't fall down. The last thing she needed was her own admittance to the hospital. She didn't want to come back to this place for a third time today, especially not as a patient.

The man's hands steadied her by her elbows. "Hey," McDermott said. "Where are you going? Is everything okay?"

The sound of his voice soothed her, but not enough to stick around. "I can't." She tried to shake herself free, but dang, McDermott was strong.

"What's wrong?" he asked, his voice carrying a definite note of panic. "Where's Taya?"

"They're inside," she said, looking up at him. Tears filled her eyes, and she hated the weakness she felt in every cell of her body. "I can't do this, McDermott. I'm not the woman you need in your life."

He clearly wasn't expecting her to say that, because he frowned and squinted at her. "What?"

"I have to go."

He let her go, and she spun away from him, her desperation today as strong as it had been in that women's clinic all those months ago.

Maybe she wasn't as healed as she thought. Maybe she would never be ready to be a wife and mother. Maybe she should just focus on repairing her family relationships before branching out to men.

She'd been making good progress there, and had attended the Fuller family dinner for the past few weeks. No one had made a big deal about her sudden reappearance, but she'd stuck to her closest allies—Berlin, Wren, and Kyler.

She hadn't really had a conversation with her mother yet, and Dawn wasn't looking forward to that. She somehow got behind the wheel of her car and started driving. The last time she'd driven with this level of emotion, she'd gone off the road. This time, she hurried home and barricaded herself in her apartment, her tears her only companions.

Chapter 9

McDermott stared after Dawn, who had a surprisingly long gait when she was determined, and then turned back to the emergency room he'd been about to enter. He had no idea what was going on with any of the women in his life, and he hated this level of helplessness.

He also hated hospitals. The last time he'd been here, it was another frantic, frustrating experience that ended with a doctor coming out of those awful plastic doors and telling him his wife was dead.

With Dawn gone, he had no way to communicate with Nana Reba, who'd surely left her phone at home, as he'd tried to call her several times without getting an answer.

He swiveled his attention back to Dawn, but she'd gotten in her car already, because he couldn't' find her blonde head.

"Taya comes first anyway," he muttered to himself. He knew it had to be so. Taya should and would always come first. He couldn't put his own selfish needs above those of his six-year-old daughter's. He wouldn't.

She needed him to be there for her, be strong, put her first. He didn't need Dawn Fuller. Though as he walked into the emergency room and scanned the seats for his grandmother, he sure would've liked her by his side. Sometimes it was hard being the strong one all the time. Sometimes he wanted to have a bad day, break down and let someone take care of him.

And not just someone. Dawn. He wanted *Dawn* to take care of him. And he wanted to take care of her.

His eyes met Nana Reba's at the same moment he realized he'd fallen in love with Dawn. Shoving that aside for the moment, he went to his grandmother. "How's Taya? What happened?"

"We haven't heard from the doctor yet." She related to him the same thing Dawn had texted. In short, she didn't know.

He said, "Stay here. I'm going to go ask," and he crossed the room to the reception desk. "Hey there, Terra. My daughter was brought in a while ago. I just got here. I need to see her. Can you check where she is for me?"

Terra clicked and tapped on the keyboard. "She's with Doctor Blanken," she said. "But McDermott, you know you can't go back there."

"Taya's six," he said. "And she's alone, and I'm all she

has." His chest lifted with the effort it took to breathe. Why couldn't he have been in town today? Filling out July's paperwork? Anything but an hour and a half away, in Dinosaur National Park, when his daughter needed him.

Terra put her hand on McDermott's and eased his fingers out of the fist they'd cinched themselves into. "Doctor Blanken is our pediatric specialist," she said. "Taya's going to be all right."

That was what he'd been told about Amelia too. His mother had said it over and over. His dad too. Her parents. And nothing in that situation had turned out all right. Flustered and panicked, McDermott turned away from Terra. "Can you go check and see how close they are to coming out?" he asked. "Maybe just find out what's wrong? We don't know anything."

"Of course. Be right back."

McDermott closed his eyes and took a deep, long breath. He prayed, as he had been the whole way here, that his daughter would be okay. That she could make a full recovery from whatever had happened.

And calm and comfort Dawn too, please, he added to the end of his pleas. Surely the Lord was tired of hearing his daily—sometimes hourly—petitions. Though Pastor Peters claimed one couldn't utter enough prayers, McDermott was starting to feel like he better slow his down or they'd stop working.

"McDermott."

He turned at the sound of Terra's voice. "Yeah?"

"She has a broken leg. They've done the x-rays, and she needs a quick surgery to reset the bones. Doctor Blanken thinks it'll be quick, nothing major. She'll come get you when she's done."

Nothing major.

McDermott managed to smile, noting the sad look of sympathy he got in response, and went to update Nana Reba. As she wept and apologized for not keeping a closer eye on Taya, McDermott pulled out his phone and texted Dawn.

Broken leg. She's going into surgery. Will probably be here for a while.

She didn't respond right away, and Nana Reba caught him looking at his phone for the sixth time. "She said she had to go to work, dear."

"Oh, right." Of course she did. Just because his daughter got injured didn't mean the banks, the post office, and the police department didn't need their garbages emptied and their floors vacuumed.

An hour passed, and it felt like a week to McDermott. His skin crawled the longer he stayed inside the walls of the hospital. "Do you want me to take you home, Nana Reba?"

"No, dear. I'm fine."

He didn't dare leave, but he couldn't stay either. "I'm just going to go stand outside for a minute," he said. "Get some fresh air. Come grab me if the doctor comes out."

Nana Reba nodded, and he escaped as fast as he

could, almost colliding with Dawn for a second time that day.

"We have to stop this," he said, relief painting everything in his life with gold and silver. He latched onto her, the scent of freshly cooked beef meeting his nose. "I need you," he whispered into her hair. "I'm so sorry if that freaks you out, but I *need* you." He buried his face against the powdery softness of her neck, glad when she stayed firm and strong and wrapped her arms around him.

She anchored him, and he wanted to blurt out how he felt about her, but he'd already said three little words that could blow up their relationship.

"I brought dinner," she finally said, her voice a touch on the strained side. He released her and backed up, noting the redness in her eyes and the way she wouldn't look straight at him.

"You didn't need to do that," he said. "I didn't mean to take you from work."

She waved her hand like she was swatting a fly. "It's your office not getting cleaned. I think you'll survive." She swept her eyes past him and toward the door. "Have you heard anything?"

He sighed. "No. And I couldn't stay in there for another second."

"I know how you feel," she said, and this time when her eyes went across his face, they hooked his. They looked at one another for several long moments, until she finally thrust the paper bag from Buffalo Bills toward him. "I brought dinner."

He took it, and though his stomach roared for the food, he didn't want to let her walk away from him again. "What did you mean when you said you weren't the woman I need?"

A storm of emotions crossed her face, and she clenched her teeth. "I am not that girl's mother."

McDermott blinked like he'd been slapped in the face. "I—"

"I don't know how to be a mother," she said. "I've never even wanted to be one. Remember how I told you I was down in Vernal to see if I was pregnant?" She glanced around and lowered her voice, her chin shaking now. "I wasn't relieved because it would've been hard to raise a baby alone. Or because I'd have to tell my mother that her 'wild child' had lived up to her reputation." Tears splashed her face, and McDermott wanted nothing more than to wipe them away and hold her against his chest until the winds had raged themselves to nothing.

"I was relieved because it meant I didn't have to be a mother. I—I—I don't know how to do it, and seeing Wren with my niece today freaked me out, and then you called, and Nana Reba almost fell, and it's...." She calmed as if by magic. "It's all too much for me, McDermott. I'm not the one for you."

Fearing he'd lose her one way or the other, he swiped his free thumb under her right eye, then her left, drawing her tears away. He kissed her on the forehead, his heart bobbing against the back of his tongue. "You're wrong," he said, his voice stuck in the back of his throat. "I need you. Just the way you are, I need you."

She let him take her into his arms, and he dropped the bag of fast food so he could hold her close. "I get there will need to be some adjustments," he whispered. "I come with a lot of extras other men don't. Heck, I don't even own my own house." He drew back just a bit and looked into Dawn's eyes, so beautiful and so full of agony.

"I can get my own place," he said. "But I'm still gonna check on Nana Reba everyday. That won't change. And of course, I can't erase my daughter."

"I know that," Dawn said.

"I'm not expecting you to be her mother," he said.

She searched his face, confusion becoming the dominant emotion in hers. "No?"

He shook his head. "No, Dawn. If we...I mean, you know, in the far distant future, if you decide we can be together, you'd be *my wife*. Not her mother."

McDermott swallowed hard, shocked and berating himself mentally for using the word wife. Dawn was already freaked out, and he didn't need to go throwing gasoline on roaring flames.

Surprisingly, she didn't turn and hightail it out of the parking lot like she had earlier.

"I will always be her dad," he said. "And I don't expect you to be her mother. Will I need your help sometimes, like today? Sure. But that doesn't mean it's for her. It's for me."

"I have no idea what I'm doing," she said. "You know that, right?"

"And I do?" He chuckled. "There's no manual you get when they send you home with a baby," he said. "Which, by the way, you didn't mention that Wren had her baby. You went to see them?"

"After lunch, yes."

"And?" She'd confessed to him that she was scared about Wren having a baby for a lot of reasons. She ran their family business, and without her, Dawn was sure everything would fall apart, or that she'd be asked to go into the office during the day.

"They looked so happy," she said wistfully.

"Babies are magical," he said. "Way different than six-year-olds."

"So you want more babies." She wasn't really asking, and while McDermott wanted to deny it, he couldn't.

"Yes," he said carefully. "I'd like to have children if I get married again."

"McDermott." Nana Reba's voice came from behind him. "The doctor's here."

He threaded his fingers through Dawn's and tugged her gently to come with him. Relieved when she did, he went inside to find out how Taya was.

CHAPTER 10

"J ust fine," Doctor Blanken must've said a dozen times. McDermott's relief wasn't hard to find, and he went back with the doctor to see his daughter though she'd likely be asleep for a few more hours due to the anesthesia.

"Come on," Dawn said to Nana Reba in the waiting room. "I'll take you home. He'll stay overnight with her." She took his grandmother home and made sure she was safely inside the house with the two dogs, McDermott's mushroom Swiss burger and fries in her hand.

Dawn stood on the front walk, gazing into the twilight, scenes from the future flashing before her in the darkening sky. If she kept dating McDermott, she knew she'd end up marrying him. Her pulse fluttered at the very thought.

Then she'd have to worry about him every morning when he left, and wonder if he was going to make it home every evening. She'd have to take care of Taya when she was well, sick, hurt, and everything in between. She wouldn't be able to work until two o'clock in the morning and sleep until eleven.

She would have to drastically change her schedule, her day-to-day activities, her whole life.

Can I do that, Lord? She tilted her head toward the heavens, but like most things, God left her to figure things out on her own. With nothing else to do, she headed over to the police station. She started working, and because she'd taken an hour and gone back to the hospital, she finished a bit later than normal.

Didn't matter. No one was at home, waiting for her. She loved Brush Creek in the dead of night, when everything was closed and everyone was at home. Even the karaoke bar was closed, and Dawn took in the stillness of the darkness, the beauty of the stars.

She hoped for clarity of thought regarding McDermott and Taya, but instead, she got the distinct impression she needed to go see her mother.

So the next morning, she slept until eleven as usual, though she'd been out an hour later than normal. She texted her mother about meeting for lunch, and her mom called, as Dawn had known she would.

"I'm at the hospital to see Baby Etta," she said, and Dawn's heart skipped a beat. "But Tate was just talking about getting lunch in the cafeteria here. You're more than welcome to come." She didn't act like it was strange that Dawn had contacted her, though Dawn certainly hadn't invited her mother to lunch in at least three years.

She didn't want to eat with Tate, though she had nothing against the man. She just couldn't say what she needed to with him there. She'd barely be able to do it without him there.

"Dawn?"

"I don't want to eat at the hospital," she said, and that was true enough. "Maybe another time."

"Wait," her mom said as if sensing Dawn was about to hang up. "What about dinner tonight? Your dad's out with Kyler tonight to get caught up on the jobs they fell behind on. You know, without Brennan, he's running himself ragged."

"He should hire someone to replace Brennan."

Her mother sighed. "He did, but Baker's taken this week off. I mean, we didn't know Wren would be having the baby; she was early you know." Her mother continued to prattle on about how the family would rally around one another, and that Brennan and Cora were doing well in California, and Dawn only had to "Hm mm," every once in a while.

"So tonight for dinner?" she asked when her mom finally took a breath. "Just you and me. I want to talk to you about something."

"Well, Berlin might come, and—"

"Just you and me, Mom," Dawn insisted. "I don't want to talk in front of Berlin, or Jazzy, or Fabi. Just you and me."

Her mom finally seemed to be listening, because a healthy pause came through the line, followed by, "All right, Dawn."

"I'll bring the food," Dawn said. "You won't even have to cook." With the plans in place, Dawn spent the next several hours obsessing about how to say anything to her mom. Pastor Peters had assured her that she didn't need to confess her sins to anyone but God.

When she showed up with Chinese food at the giant house where she'd grown up, it took all her courage and all her willpower to go inside. None of the children lived there anymore, but her parents would never sell the place. The Fuller mansion had been in their family since the beginning of Brush Creek history, and they planned to keep it that way.

"Mom?" she called when she went inside.

"In the kitchen," her mom yelled back. Dawn maneuvered through the furniture in the great room and set the food on the dining room table.

"The blue looks nice," she said, noting the new color on the walls in the kitchen, where her mom pulled plates out of the cupboard. She turned, and all the blue eyes and blonde features in the Fuller family belonged to her. Of course, since Dawn's dad was also towheaded with bright blue eyes, all the Fullers had some shade of blue and a range of blondes from dirty dishwater blonde to Fabi's cornsilk-colored hair.

Dawn moved the food to the kitchen counter, and

they dished up the things they wanted. "So," her mom said. "How are things with McDermott?"

Dawn hadn't expressly told her parents about her relationship with McDermott, but they had eyes. They could see she sat by him at church, and surely Kyler had said something about the two of them even though she'd asked him not to.

"I don't know." Dawn sighed, spearing a piece of broccoli with a slice of beef.

"He's a nice man," her mother said. "Very handsome. Cute little girl. Stable job, right here in town." Her mom cast a sideways look at her, and Dawn found herself nodding along.

"He's all of that," she agreed.

"You like him, yes?"

"Very much," Dawn said, her food sticking in her throat. Her mom seemed pleased about that, and Dawn could only imagine how many steps up McDermott was from the other men she'd dated. Probably several stories, which made his attraction to her completely insane.

"He's completely smitten with you." Her mom giggled.

"How do you know?"

"Oh, Kyler says he's talkin' about you all the time. Dawn this and Dawn that."

Dawn put her fork down, unable to put another bite in her mouth. "I think I have to break up with him."

"What? Why would you do that?" Her mom paused, her fork hanging in midair.

"He's…it's complicated." She didn't want to voice her selfishness. Tell her mother that she wasn't ready to be a mother. All her mom had ever wanted was to be a mother—and she'd done just that nine times. *Nine.*

"Dawn, I get you've had a rough year or so, but—"

"I don't want children, Mom," Dawn blurted out. As she suspected, her mom's face contorted with horror, like such a thing was unfathomable. "And he comes with a child. I'd have no choice." Dawn hadn't come here to tell her mom this, but all her fears and worries about McDermott and Taya spilled from her.

Her mom didn't offer any advice, the way Dawn had been hoping she would. She didn't tell Dawn what she should do, which Dawn desperately wanted someone to do.

"You'll figure it out," her mom said, patting her hand and happily munching on the last egg roll.

Dawn managed to squeeze down another couple of bites of sweet and sour chicken and then let her mom pack up the leftovers, knowing she'd never eat them. But she took them, hugged her mom—something she hadn't done in a while—and went to get ready for work.

———

OUT OF THE four buildings she cleaned, Dawn disliked the post office the most. They produced the most trash, and all the walls and floors were white, which meant they showed the most dirt.

So she cleaned the post office first each evening, just to get the worst one out of the way. She went to the police station second and saved the two banks in town for last. They had the best security systems and the brightest lights, and someone always had a sweet-smelling candle they'd been burning during the day.

As she loaded the trash from the police station all into one big can, the front door opened and someone entered. It wasn't abnormal for that to happen, as the station had a pair of policemen on the premises, even in the middle of the night.

But Dawn knew it wasn't one of them. Sure enough, McDermott stood there, that sexy smile on his face. They'd left things on good terms, but Dawn's inner turmoil had been churning for twenty-four hours.

"Hey," he said.

She positioned the huge trash can between them. "How's Taya?"

"She's at home, recovering."

"What are you doing here, then?"

"I didn't come in today, so I came to get some files." He approached her, and Dawn's heart leapt around inside her chest like an angry frog. He paused to kiss her, but Dawn put one hand on his chest.

"I don't—" Dawn's voice broke.

McDermott looked at her, his questions fading to resignation. "What can I do to change your mind?"

She shook her head, her silent *Nothing this time,*

easily communicated to him. Because this wasn't about him. It was about her.

"It's my fault," she said. "I wasn't ready to start dating, and I said yes to you anyway. And you're...you're wonderful, and I'm...I'm not...ready."

He cocked his head to the side, a look of disbelief on his face. "Don't do this."

"I'm done here. I'll leave you to work."

"You know I didn't come here to work."

He'd come to see her, the way he probably always had over the past fifteen months. "McDermott—"

"You can have as much time as you need. I've never pushed you to move faster than you want to move."

"What if I'm never ready?" she cried, shaking her head. "Sorry, McDermott. I'm so sorry." She pushed her trashcan toward the front of the building, expecting him to call her back, beg her to reconsider, offer her more wonderful things in his sultry, smooth voice.

He didn't.

CHAPTER 11

McDermott couldn't hide his frustration and disappointment about Dawn's disappearance from his life. Even something as simple as making coffee in the morning required extra banging and slamming of mugs and sugar bowls.

"What's eating you?" Nana Reba asked, placing her hands on her hips.

"Nothing," he said darkly adding more cream to his coffee than he normally did. He spit the offending drink into the sink and sighed. "You'll be okay with Taya today?"

"Yeah, sure," she said. "She'll be up and running with those dogs before you know it."

"I can take another day off." He could take a week off. Or two. He had enough vacation saved up for a month of time off.

"Not necessary. By the way you abused that coffee

pot, I think you're probably ready to get outside of these walls."

If that was the only thing McDermott needed, he'd have agreed, kissed his grandmother's forehead, and gone to work for half the day before coming back to take care of his daughter.

"Yeah. Gotta get outside these walls." He turned from the window, the mended cracks in his heart opening again. She wasn't Amelia, but he didn't need her to be. He had room in his heart to love again, and he had, and now he didn't know what to do with that gaping hole Dawn had left behind.

Fill the hole.

He wasn't sure where the voice came from, or even if it was his own. He wasn't sure what it meant, or how to do it. But he pulled out his phone and messaged Dawn. She wouldn't be up for hours, but he couldn't wait.

Meet for lunch?

He wanted to explain he was only working for half the day and he'd meet her anywhere. But he thought short and simple would be better, and all he could do was hope and pray that she wouldn't ignore him.

He drove his route, pulled over people speeding, and parked next to the high school when he saw a truckload of teenagers heading up to the baseball fields. Nothing happened. Hardly anything did in Brush Creek.

Eleven o'clock came and went and he still didn't have a text from Dawn. By noon, he'd have eaten anything just to get the jittery feeling out of his gut. He chose Ruby's

Roost, because he could sit at the bar and pretend like he wasn't alone. He'd see locals and old friends, and he could make believe that his girlfriend hadn't left him for seemingly no reason.

What if I'm never ready?

Her words haunted him, and he took an extra moment in his cruiser before going into the Roost to pray that the Lord would heal Dawn's heart, erase her past, help her see that McDermott wasn't the enemy.

He'd just sat down and ordered his bacon cheeseburger when his phone buzzed. *I'm at the office today. It's so boring here and I had to be here at nine.*

Though he could hear her displeasure just from reading the words, a smile bloomed on his face.

I can bring you something.

Not necessary. A picture came through—a brown sack lunch that she'd drawn a purple smiley face on. *I'll text you later.*

And that was that.

McDermott stared at his phone, wondering what he should do. He knew where she was. He knew she liked cinnamon more than chocolate. He knew the bakery made the best oatmeal raisin cookies on the planet, and that they satisfied her cinnamon craving.

"This seat taken?"

He glanced over as Kyler slid onto the stool. He stared at this new version of his best friend, one with a short, military-style haircut and a clean-shaven face. "What happened to you?"

Kyler chuckled and looked at the menu though he had it memorized. "Starlee happened to me."

"You're going out with Starlee Riggs?"

"No, she cut my hair." Kyler shook his head. "Starlee's engaged." He cut McDermott a look out of the corner of his eye. "You didn't know?"

McDermott cleared his throat and lifted his root beer to his lips. "I don't keep up with town gossip as well as you."

Kyler ordered the ham and triple cheese omelet and twisted toward McDermott. "I think I'm ready to…I don't know. My mother says 'move on'. Guess I'm ready to do that."

"That's great," McDermott said, wishing his smile was a little more genuine. "Did you meet someone that sparked your interest?"

"Not yet." He cocked his head at McDermott. "How do I do that?"

McDermott laughed. A real, actual laugh and not a forced one. "I have no idea."

"Oh, that's right. You've had your eye on my sister for a while."

McDermott shook his head, a chuckle coming out despite his miserable conditions. "She broke up with me."

"She—what?"

"Last night."

"Why?"

"Your sister had a baby and my daughter broke her leg."

Kyler blinked, the two obviously not adding up to a break-up. McDermott didn't want to explain. His food came, and he dug into it.

"I'll talk to her."

"I don't need you to do that." McDermott shook his head. He didn't know what he needed anyone to do. But Dawn had texted him back, and he held onto the hope that maybe, just maybe, she'd figure out that she needed him too, whether she was ready for it or not.

———

MCDERMOTT LEARNED how to survive without a guarantee of hearing from Dawn on a daily basis. His daughter's leg healed, and summer faded into fall. Taya skipped off to first grade happily, hardly a stitch in her stride, and McDermott squeezed Nana Reba's hand.

"So, what are you gonna do all day?" he asked her.

"Oh, those two mongrels of yours take so much energy."

McDermott tossed his head back and laughed. "I'll give you Louise. She's a big troublemaker. But Thelma? She'd feel bad if she knew what you'd just said."

Nana Reba grinned at him. "I'm headed up to the fields this morning. We're doing the recycling of the old boxes today."

McDermott had never been happier that he had another job to go to, that he couldn't go help with the recycling. He'd done it more times than he could count as a boy growing up, and walking through the fields to collect old, wet, and partially decomposed cardboard was definitely not fun.

"I heard something at church yesterday," Nana Reba said as they made their way back to the car.

"Oh yeah?"

"Rumors, I'm sure."

"Well, we don't care about rumors," he said. "You taught me that, Nana." It was something she'd told him every day from the time he was fourteen until the day he graduated from high school. For the most part, McDermott had managed to live drama-free, even when people whispered about him after Amelia's death.

"Of course, of course." She paused before getting in his cruiser so he could take her home and get to work. "And I don't believe this anyway, because you would've told me."

McDermott waited for her to say what she wanted to. She would no matter what. "Go on, then."

"You broke up with Dawn?"

"She broke up with me."

"When?"

McDermott sighed. "I don't know." But he knew the exact day. Even if Taya hadn't broken her leg that day, he'd remember. "Several weeks ago."

"But you still go out at night."

"I need to meet someone else, don't I?"

"Oh, pshaw," she said, slapping his chest. "You don't want to meet anyone else."

"I can't make her like me, Nana."

"She likes you. And you—you're in love with her."

"I go to my office a lot too," he said, ignoring Nana's words. He'd also been meeting Kyler and discussing strategies for him to meet new women in town. Kyler had been out of the dating scene for three years, and they were still working on a plan for Kyler to get introduced to one of the new third grade teachers who'd come to town.

"So you see Dawn still."

He didn't want to admit it, but yes, he'd seen her. He hadn't spoken to her, and if she'd seen his cruiser in the parking lot as he waited for her to finish her job at the station, she'd never texted to say so. Once, she looked right at him. Neither of them had moved, and then she'd continued taking the trash out.

He'd go in after she left, just to catch a whiff of her perfume. Just to imagine he could touch the same surfaces she had. She looked tired, and she'd started wearing her hair up.

Over the past couple of months since they'd broken up, she'd texted him back every time he'd dared send her a message. He was trying to fill the hole she'd left behind with whatever pieces of her he could find, anything she would give him.

"No, Nana," he said. "I don't talk to her."

"Are you telling me you're stalking her?"

"Sh." He looked around and opened the door for his grandmother. "Get in." The last thing he needed was his reputation as a state trooper being tarnished by gossip about stalking.

"I go to work, and I wait for her to leave so it's not awkward for her," he said once he'd slid behind the wheel and closed the door. "It's not stalking." He started the short drive back to the cul-de-sac so he could finish this conversation.

Nana Reba wrung her hands. "Well, I don't know what to do now."

"Why do you need to do anything?" McDermott pulled into the driveway and put the cruiser in park.

"I was just so sure you'd end up together."

"I haven't given up hope yet," McDermott said.

"You haven't?"

"She just needs more time. And not time while we're together. But time where she can work through whatever she needs to." As he spoke, he realized how right he was. And he sent another prayer heavenward that Dawn could be blessed with clarity of mind and the knowledge that she was already everything she needed to be.

"Now go on," he said. "I've got to get to work."

Nana Reba looked at him for several more seconds, then leaned over and kissed his cheek. "You're a good boy, McDermott. She'll come around." She got out and moved slowly up the walk and into the house, her words sparking an additional measure of hope in McDermott.

CHAPTER 12

*T*aya's first day of first grade.

Dawn read McDermott's text, wishing her heartbeat didn't zing around inside her body like a ping pong ball every time her phone chimed. She also wished she hadn't been getting up at eight AM for the past seven weeks, but she had been.

Wren should be back to work next week in the office, and Dawn couldn't wait. She was basically working two full-time jobs, and trying to grapple with the loneliness that had descended on her the moment she'd cast McDermott from her life.

He texted her from time to time. No set schedule. It seemed like he felt like he wanted to keep her up to date with the most important happenings in his life, like his daughter's first day of school.

Dawn had responded to all of his messages, mostly because she had no desire to hurt him further than she was sure she had. "You want to keep the door open," she muttered to herself, which was also selfish and unfair to him.

Still, she thumbed out a response to him. *How's her leg?*

All healed, he responded. It was a light break. Easy surgery. She did just fine with it.

Dawn left the messages there, and McDermott would too. At least until next time he sent her something. Sometimes she found a bag of oatmeal raisin cookies outside her door, and she knew he'd been there. He couldn't help running her fingers along the doorknob, wondering if he'd touched it.

And he came to the police station every night. He never came in, which she appreciated but which also drove her bananas. Was he just trying to give her breathing room? Did he not want her back in his life?

He probably just didn't want to get his heart stomped on again. She answered the company phone when it rang, and she texted Wren when her sister asked if she could come in later that week to get caught up on everything that Dawn had done at A Jack of All Trades for the past several weeks.

The truth was, Dawn felt lost. Not in the same, spiritual way as she had after her accident last year. But in a physical, what-do-I-want-from-my-life? kind of way. She'd never had to question what she'd do for a job. She'd grown up in the family business, and when she'd been offered the nightly commercial cleaning, she'd seized onto it and never let go. She liked it.

It wasn't a career change she needed. She just wasn't sure a typical, suburban life would fit in with her job.

Maybe she didn't want it to.

She'd tried praying and listening at church for answers. It seemed as if God had finally tired of her, and she'd taken His silence to mean *Figure it out, Dawn.*

But she didn't know how.

And every day that passed, she worried that McDermott would meet someone new who was dying to be a mother, a wife, and a two-dog walker. He'd dated before her, she knew.

She'd told no one about the break-up, though she went to the family dinners every week.

On Wednesday when she showed up with a sack of chocolate chip cookies from the bakery, Wren gave her a side-hug. "The bakery, huh?"

"Well, some of us don't have time to bake now that they're working two jobs."

Wren smiled, but ever since she'd had Etta, she'd seemed tired. Her hair had changed color, and the texture was more like straw than anything else. Dawn's selfish side reared it's ugly head once more. She didn't want to trade in certain aspects of her life, though Etta was a cute little thing that made the sweetest noises.

Wren held the baby now and said, "I'm so glad she's sleeping. Hopefully, she'll be napping when I come tomorrow too."

"Does she not sleep at night?" Their mother joined the conversation from her position at the stove, where she had three pans of potatoes frying.

"Not really, no." Wren bounced Etta the teensiest bit. "She thinks nighttime is the best time to be awake."

Dawn agreed with the baby, actually, but she wanted to sleep when she wanted to, not when an eight-pound human let her. She turned away from Wren, wishing she could turn away from her own thoughts as easily.

"When are you going to invite McDermott to meet the family?" Wren asked.

Dawn blinked, and when she opened her eyes, all she saw was white for a moment. Her mother said nothing, but the woman had ears like a bat. She could maneuver in the dark toward any sound and understand words that had been whispered from across the room. Dawn supposed raising nine children could develop keen hearing for a person.

Dawn turned back to Wren, glad no one else was in the kitchen for now. "Um, I'm not seeing him anymore."

Her mother dropped the spatula she'd been using at the same time Wren's eyes widened. "What? Why not? You guys were so good together." Wren seemed honestly confused.

"It's...I don't know," Dawn said lamely. If her father were in the room, she'd never be able to get away with "I don't know." If any of the kids ever said that, he'd said, "That's not an answer. Think about it. You know."

And she did know why she'd ended her relationship with McDermott. She just didn't want to say it out loud.

But Wren was staring at her, and the potatoes were going to be extra-crispy for dinner, as her mom hadn't even attempted to pick up the spatula she'd dropped, nor had she moved to get out another one.

"Look," she said, flustered and annoyed that she had to answer to her mom and perfect older sister. "I'm not like you, Wren. I'm never going to meet the man of my dreams and have babies and be a wonderful mother."

Wren opened her mouth and then closed it again.

"Dawn—" her mother started.

"I'm the wild child, Mom. Isn't that what you always say? Well, I don't want the plain, boring suburban life McDermott has to offer. Plain as that." If only she didn't feel like she'd just told the largest lie on the planet.

She did want love. And stability. *And* the ability to roam free. Get outside the typical stereotype of what a family should look like. Because with McDermott, she'd never have the typical family.

The front door opened and the twins walked in, babbling to each other about an online shoe sale and if the website offered free returns or not.

"I'm going to go," Dawn said. "You can keep the cookies."

"Don't go," her mom said at the same time Wren said, "You don't need to leave."

But Dawn didn't want to be there. Didn't want to endure their helpless, sympathetic looks. Didn't want to continue the conversation, especially not with more ears present.

"I'm not mad," she said, which made Jazzy and Fabi stop talking. "Hey, guys." She turned to them and used a falsely bright voice. "I just had something come up, so I'm gonna head out."

She got her feet moving, knowing she could escape if she just got going. Behind her, Wren said something but Dawn didn't wait. She'd just unlocked her car when Wren came out the front door, babyless.

"Dawn, wait." She approached slower when she realized Dawn wasn't going to get in her car and drive off. "I'm not even close to a wonderful mother."

Dawn cinched her teeth together. There was no point in making Wren feel bad because she did all the right things.

"Mom rides me constantly." Wren sighed and scraped her bangs off her forehead. "Nothing I do with Etta is right. I can't even get her to sleep at night. I mean, people sleep at night, don't they?"

For the first time, Dawn took a moment to hear Wren's frustration and realize that she had struggles and troubles of her own. Maybe she made everything she did look effortless, but that didn't mean it was.

"If you go, then I have to deal with the twins alone. Berlin isn't coming, and I can't handle Jazzy and Fabi while they're talking about fashion." The twins had wanted to be fashion designers from the moment they were born, if their mother was to be believed. They both sewed everything they wore, and Dawn had always seen it as another way they excelled while she failed.

"I'm not up for talking about McDermott." Dawn folded her arms. She couldn't believe she was even considering going back inside for the family dinner.

"Nope." Wren shook her head. "No talking about McDreamy. I mean, McDermott." She grinned at Dawn and waved back toward the house. "Come on, they were already arguing about a wedge-heeled sandal when I left."

———

WREN HAD BEEN true to her word and kept her mouth shut about McDermott during dinner. But when she showed up at the office the next day with her sleeping baby, the first thing she said was, "Tate said McDermott's been in a funk for weeks. How long ago did you guys break up?"

"Couple of months now," Dawn said.

"And you didn't tell me?" Wren seemed genuinely hurt.

"You've been busy with the baby. Dawn pulled out the folder she'd prepared for this meeting. "Okay, so we have four new clients on the residential maid service that Jazzy and Fabi have been doing. When I booked the last one, you should've heard Jazzy freak out."

Wren shook her head as she scanned the new accounts and family names Dawn had added to their clientele. "She acts like working six hours a day is too much."

"She should try doing it between eight PM and two AM," Dawn said.

"You don't like the commercial schedule?" Wren peered at her with concern in her eyes.

"No, I love it." She sighed and sat at the desk. "I didn't get any new commercial businesses, so you'll have to add that to the September goals."

"Honestly, we can't handle any more clients without hiring more people." She perched on the edge of the desk and ignored the folder. "And every time I ask Dad about that, he says he won't do it. 'Family only.'"

"Which is why he and Kyler are killing themselves and working seven days a week." Dawn shook her head. "They have to replace Brennan. He worked full time just on the rec center and schools."

"No one wants to work as hard as we do for our business. They've hired and lost two guys."

Wren went through the accounts receivable and payable and told Dawn that she'd done a great job. "Are you happy you won't have to man this desk anymore?"

"Truthfully, it hasn't been too bad. Combined with my commercial cleaning, it's tough. But if this was all I did, it wouldn't be so bad."

Wren nodded, her expression thoughtful. "What really happened with you and McDermott? He's not happy, and you're obviously not either."

Dawn folded her arms and looked at her sister. "He's

been married before. He has a daughter. And I don't want to be a mother." She ticked the items off on her fingers as she spoke. "So there're three strikes against him. Oh, and he lives with his grandmother. Four strikes. He's out."

She sounded callous and what she'd said was utterly ridiculous. But Wren took a few moments to ponder it, and Dawn appreciated that.

"He shouldn't get a strike for being a widower," she said.

"He'll never love me as much as Amelia."

"So what?" Wren challenged. " He doesn't have to love you as much or more. He just has to love you." She spoke softly, but her eyes held great power. "Do you think he loves you?"

"I don't know," Dawn said again, though at certain moments during her relationship with McDermott she'd certainly felt loved.

"He gets a pass for the daughter too," Wren said. "He can't just get rid of her because you don't want her."

"I didn't say I didn't want her," Dawn said. "I love Taya. She's a great kid."

"He can buy a new house." Wren held up four fingers and put three of them down. "I'll give you that you don't want to be a mother. But don't you think that's a strike against *you*? Not him?"

Dawn blinked. "I've made a lot of mistakes in my life." And McDermott hadn't judged her for any of them.

"Don't make him one of them." Wren lifted one shoulder as if to say, *That's all I'm sayin'.* Then she picked up her baby carrier and balanced it on her hip. "I've got to go. You can sleep in again on Monday. I know you like your beauty rest." She gave Dawn a quick smile and left the office.

Dawn stared after her. Don't make him one of your mistakes.

She couldn't get her phone out fast enough.

CHAPTER 13

McDermott had just written a ticket, meeting his quota for September, when his phone rang. "Hey, Nana," he said after he picked up.

"I think you need to get over to the station," she said.

He frowned and cocked his head toward the radio. It hadn't gone off, and if the police department in Brush Creek needed him, they knew how to get ahold of him. "Why's that?"

When she didn't answer, every mental red flag McDermott possessed went up. "Nana?" He drew her name out slowly, quickly calculating how long it would take him to get back to Brush Creek. He'd been patrolling north and west today, and he was probably twenty minutes from the station. Twenty-five from the elementary school.

"Is Taya okay?"

"Taya's fine," she said a bit evasively.

"Then why do I need to go to the station?" He'd been dropping Taya at school and then going to work, which was about an hour later than he normally did. Nana Reba picked her up and he made it home about six, just in time for dinner.

Once Taya was in bed, he ran over to the station in time to catch a glimpse of Dawn, but she'd been gone the last three nights. He didn't want to admit that his heart had taken a beating, that he'd driven by her apartment over the bookstore just to see if there were any lights on.

There had been, and he wondered if she was sick. If she needed help. If maybe cookies would be welcome. She'd told him once that cookies would always be welcome, but he hadn't stopped by the bakery yet.

"Nana, if you can't give me a reason to come to the station, I have work to do out on the highways."

She exhaled like he was being the most difficult man on the planet. "When's your paperwork day?"

"Not until the new month," he said, watching as a motorist slowed when they saw him parked on the side of the road.

"All right. I'll tell her."

"Tell who?"

"Gotta go." The line went dead and McDermott stared at his cell, completely bewildered. When he got home, Nana Reba was asleep on the couch. Or at least she pretended to be. McDermott narrowed his eyes at her, trying to determine if her breathing was a fake slow or if she was actually asleep.

Taya skipped into the room and said, "Daddy! Come see what I made at school." She put her tiny hand in his and tugged him into the kitchen. Dinner in the form of hamburgers and fruit sat on the counter, and he put together a bun with mayo, ketchup, and mustard as Taya talked a mile a minute about the painting she'd made.

"It's watercolors, Daddy. And I put the black on first, and the water didn't stick to it, like how we do the Easter eggs."

He grinned at her. "Looks great, baby. Did you eat dinner?"

"Yep. Nana said she was real tired because they closed up the fields today."

"Ah, I see." And yet, she still had time to call him about nonsensical things.

"She said there's salad in the fridge."

"Lettuce salad or potato salad?" He was only interested in the non-green stuff, and Taya opened the fridge and pulled out a plastic container.

"Potato. I helped peel the eggs."

"You don't say." He beamed at her because she seemed so proud at herself.

"Daddy?"

"Yeah, baby?"

"Why doesn't Dawn come over anymore? I asked Nana Reba, but she said she didn't know."

McDermott put his hamburger down and finished

chewing, trying to find the right words for a six-year-old. "Remember how I said we were dating?"

She nodded, her innocent blue eyes wide. She'd believe anything he told her. So he chose his next words carefully. "Sometimes, when people do that, they're learning about each other. You know, to see if they like each other. Like when you make a new friend."

"Like Kara."

He snapped his fingers and pointed at his daughter. "Just like that. She told you about her pup, and you told her about Thelma and Louise, and you get along." He took a long breath. "So that's what me and Dawn were doing. And we were gettin' along, and...." His voice trailed off, because he didn't know how to tell his daughter that Dawn wasn't ready. He barely understood it himself.

He'd never stopped to consider if he was ready to be a father. And certainly no one had asked him if he was ready to be a widower and a single dad.

"Did you get in a fight?" Taya asked.

"Sort of," he said. "We still talk a little. I think we'll get back together...eventually."

"What does that mean?"

"It means sooner or later."

Taya nodded, though McDermott knew that wasn't a great explanation either. "I liked her."

"I did too," McDermott said, pinching off a piece of his meat to feed to Thelma. "I did too."

———

WHEN DAWN WASN'T at the police station for a fourth night in a row, his heart sank down to the toes of his boots. Maybe she'd changed her schedule so she cleaned it later. Or earlier. No matter what, it was a very clear message that said, *Leave me alone, McDermott.*

But somehow, he couldn't do it.

He placed a call and stared at the entrance to the police station while the line rang.

"McDermott?" Walker asked, clearly confused. "What's goin' on? You okay?"

"Fine," he said. "I'm so sorry. I just realized how late it is." And for a cowboy like Walker who got up early, nine-thirty might as well be midnight.

He yawned. "It's fine. Haven't seen you up here in the several weeks."

He hadn't been able to go since school started. They hadn't gone while Taya's leg healed either. "Yeah, or I'd have mentioned that Dawn and I broke up."

"I know that. You've been sittin' alone at church."

"Right. So I've, uh, been seeing her at the police station. She cleans it at night, and I go in sometimes after Taya goes to bed, you know?" He cleared his throat. "So anyway, she hasn't been here the last four nights."

"It's McDermott," Walker said, half into the receiver and half not. "I'm askin' 'im." His voice was louder when he said, "Tess wants to know what's goin' on with you two. Anyway, where do you think she is?"

"I don't know. Should I call her?"

"What did you do last time you wanted to get her attention? Get a real answer?"

"I called her."

"There you go."

Pure fear struck him behind the ribs. "I think if I do, and it's the wrong thing to do, it will be the end for us."

"But what if it's the right thing to do?"

"Call her," Tess yelled from somewhere on the other end of the line.

"Why'd you guys break up?"

"Oh, she's not ready for all the complications I bring to the table." He wouldn't have to explain more than that to Walker. Thankfully.

"Call her. Then you better at least text me back so Tess can sleep tonight." Scuffling came through the line, followed by both of them laughing, and McDermott basked in the sound of it for just a moment.

With one call done, and another to be made, McDermott gathered his wits about him. He'd had to sequester himself in his closet the first time he'd called Dawn and practically demanded what it would take to get her to go out with him.

"What should I say this time?" he asked the Lord. Nothing definitive came to mind, so he did the only thing he'd been able to rely on since Amelia's death.

He acted, trusting in his faith that the words would come.

Her line rang once, twice, three times. In the middle

of the fourth ring, he felt sure the call would go to voice-mail. Then her beautiful voice said, "Hello?"

"Oh, hey," he said as if he hadn't intentionally dialed her number. He took a deep breath and launched right into it. "I haven't seen you at the station in a few nights, and I was worried maybe you've been sick."

"I'm fine."

"I...miss you."

She sighed, but he couldn't tell if it was borne from exasperation or if it was the soft, sweet sigh he'd heard her give after he kissed her. "Hey, can I call you tomorrow? I'm really busy right now."

He strained to hear something in the background that would tell him where she was. He heard nothing. "Yeah, sure," he finally said.

"Great, talk to you later." She hung up, and he stared out the windshield. He needed to see her every day. It had been the only thing keeping him sane these past nine weeks they'd been apart. But without another choice, he eased the cruiser on home and went to bed.

———

THE NEXT EVENING, he paced on the back patio, trying to keep himself from going over to the police station. "She won't be there anyway," he told himself. A cold front had blown in that morning, and he really just wanted to go to bed.

But Dawn hadn't called, and McDermott's last thread of hope was almost frayed.

It's ten minutes, he told himself. Five there just to see if her car was outside. Five back if it wasn't. He could certainly spare ten minutes, couldn't he?

For Dawn, he could spare almost anything, so he went inside, grabbed his leather jacket, and said to Nana Reba, "I'll be back in a few minutes."

She nodded without looking up from her knitting. Even when he'd questioned her about the phone call yesterday, she'd been very tight lipped and had refused to say anything. There was something afoot, and the state trooper in him would figure it out eventually.

He turned from Main to Park, only a couple more blocks separating him from the police station. If she wasn't there, he didn't know what he'd do. Probably go stake out her place until she showed up and he could talk to her.

As Oxbow Park eased past on his right, he became aware that something was different about the police station. All the lights were off inside, and that never happened. The building sat shrouded in darkness, and he thought sure the power had gone out. But the fire department next door was lit from inside, and all the street-lamps in the parking lot seemed to be working fine too.

He reached for his radio and said, "Hey, so I'm heading into my office to grab a few files, and all the lights are out. James, are you there?"

Only silence came back. He didn't have his weapon

with him, and he reasoned that he probably didn't need one. This was a simple electrical failure.

Still, he parked so his headlights shone on the front doors, and he approached the entrance slowly. His phone rang, making him nearly jump out of his skin. He fumbled the device, especially when he saw Dawn's name on the screen.

"Hey," he breathed, still trying to see inside the dark station.

"Where are you?" she asked.

"At the police station."

A beat passed and then she said, "Stalking me again, I see."

"You haven't been here for days," he said.

"Then why are you there?"

"A fool's hope," he said. "I was just tryin' to decide if camping outside the bookstore would be considered inappropriate."

"Are you coming in?"

McDermott paused, her words taking their sweet time to click around inside his head. "You're inside?"

She didn't answer, and when he checked his phone, he found that the call had been disconnected. With his heart throbbing with hope now—and fine, still a little bit of trepidation—he entered the police station.

The lights blazed to life and James stood from behind the dispatch desk. "Surprise," he boomed, his gaze flying to McDermott's office door—which was closed. He walked toward McDermott. "She said I could have a long lunch break, so I'm gonna take that now." He clapped McDermott on the shoulder and grinned as he passed.

His door opened and Dawn stood there in all her glory. Those blue eyes. That honeyed hair in those loose waves. Every cell in his body wanted to touch her, and he barely got his brain in control before he flew across the room and kissed her.

"You sent James on a long lunch?" McDermott paused a healthy ten feet from her.

"He said the chief wouldn't mind." She waved him toward her, a timid smile on her lips. "Come on in."

He followed her into his office, and she closed the door before pressing her back into it. "First, thank you for all the cookies. I'm sure I'm ten pounds heavier because of you."

He nodded and spotted a box on his desk. "What's this?"

"My mother and I spent the afternoon making that for you. I believe you said chocolate was your favorite dessert." She inched closer to him. So close he caught the scent of her perfume, the soft, powdery smell he'd missed so intensely.

He lifted the lid on the cake box and sucked in a breath. The chocolate cake in the box looked like a professional pastry chef had labored over it for hours. The frosting had been perfectly peaked, with a silver ball at the top of each spike.

"This is beautiful," he said. "But it's not my birthday."

"It's mine," she said, causing his eyes to fly to hers. His heart wailed in his chest. He couldn't miss her birthday, and he didn't have anything to give her.

Her hand touched his, and he was so startled that he yanked his back.

"Okay, I've freaked you out," she said. "Just one more thing I'm not good at."

"What aren't you good at?"

"I'm trying to make up with you," she said. "Get you back. I'm terribly lonely without you, and I don't want you to be one of my mistakes."

He had no idea what she was talking about, and his face must've sent that message. She closed her eyes and drew in a deep breath. When she looked at him again, her eyes swam with tears, with hope, with determination.

"I'm sorry, McDermott. I love you, and all I want for my birthday is to have one more kiss with you."

He blinked, sure he must be dreaming. Had she said she loved him? His ears rang, and the word *love* bounced around inside his eardrums.

"I think we can have more than one," he whispered. "I mean, if you love me and all."

She ran her fingers up his arms, and he cupped her face in his hands. "Happy birthday," he said just before touching his lips to hers. It might as well have been his birthday, because all of his wishes came true in that single kiss.

CHAPTER 14

Dawn memorized the feel of McDermott's hands on her face. The taste of his mouth like the coffee he drank after dinner. "I'm so sorry," she whispered against his lips.

"Doesn't matter," he said, his voice husky. He kissed her cheek, the soft skin by her ear. "Honestly, Dawn. When I watched you walk out of this office, I knew you'd be back." He pulled away and looked at her. "We're meant to be, you and I."

"Oh, you think so?" She smiled at him, so very happy to see him grinning back.

"You're my treasure," he said, his love and adoration for her evident in his tone, his eyes. "I love you."

She kissed him again, knowing she'd have a lot more explaining to do. Sure enough, he backed off soon after that and wanted to eat the cake and get some answers.

"What made you decide you were ready?" he asked.

"I'm still not ready," she said. "But I don't think I need to be. God doesn't wait for people to be perfect to put them where He needs them. My mom didn't make this cake perfectly the first time she tried. Wren can't get her baby to sleep at night." She shrugged, hoping all the weird pieces she'd just said would make sense to him.

"If I wait until I'm sure I'm ready, I'll never—I mean —that's not what living is. Living is messy. Living is making mistakes and trying to fix them the next time. You know?" She watched him, and while he seemed a bit confused, he nodded.

"This cake is fantastic. So however many times she had to practice, it was worth it."

Dawn giggled as he took another huge bite. "I'm twenty-eight today," she said. "And all I could think about was you. I came to the station a couple of days ago to tell you, but you weren't here."

He stalled in his cake consumption. "Is that why Nana Reba called me and told me I needed to come to the station?"

Dawn nodded, forking off a more delicate bite of cake. "I still got you here."

He looked straight at her, straight into her soul. "Dawn, I would go anywhere to be with you."

She ducked her head, her curls falling between them. Heat rose to her face, and she said, "It was Wren having her baby that freaked me out and made me break up with you. And it was Wren making mistakes as she mothered her baby that made me realize I'd rather make mistakes with you than not have you at all."

"I thought you just said you didn't want me to be one of your mistakes."

"Right. I've made some mistakes in my life, and they're what make me, well, me. But I didn't want losing you to be one of my mistakes." She hoped she was making sense.

He grinned and dragged his fork through the frosting on top of his cake. With a mischievous glint in his eye, his hand darted out and dabbed the frosting on her nose. "Oops. My mistake."

He laughed, abandoning his cake to kiss the sweet from her face, working his way to her lips. "I hope we make a lot of mistakes together, sweetheart."

"Me too, McDermott. Me too."

———

MEMORIAL DAY, nine months later:

"It's windy," Wren said as she fiddled with the fine buttons on the back of Dawn's wedding dress. "Your updo is going to be a down-do in only a few minutes."

"It's okay," she said. Brennan's wedding had been moved inside the fire station at the very last minute. Wren had warned Dawn away from May, claiming the weather was still too unpredictable. But she and McDermott wanted to get married on a meaningful day. He wanted to make a sad day happy, and she wanted to get married when it wasn't a hundred degrees outside.

Memorial Day was the perfect day, and if the wind wasn't howling up at the horse farm, everything would go off without a hitch.

"Is it going to rain?" her mom asked.

"Not a cloud in the sky," Wren said. "It's just windy up here. Landon says it gets like this in the spring." She speared Dawn with a look that said *I told you summer would've been better.*

Dawn ignored her and tucked a loose curl into her updo. "Spray that piece again, Berlin."

Her sister complied, and Dawn's stomach flipped over when she reminded herself that she was getting married today. She would be a mom in about an hour. Her whole life would change, and instead of being upset or nervous about it, she felt...ready.

Ready to embrace whatever life threw at her. Ready to do the best she could with Taya. Ready to lean on McDermott if things got hard, and support him when he needed it.

Her sister sprayed her hair and said, "You're beautiful, Dawn."

The sisters hugged, and Berlin said, "I wish I was coming to Cozumel with you. Are you sure you don't need a nanny?"

"Nana Reba is coming," Dawn said, laughing. "She's

so worked up about McDermott and Taya moving out, even though we'll literally be three houses down the street." She shook her head, though she loved Nana Reba and was glad McDermott had found a house so close to his grandmother. He needed to be able to look after her, and he didn't want to disrupt everything in Taya's life.

They'd worked out a schedule of sorts. Once school started again in the fall, McDermott would take Taya to school. Dawn would pick her up twice a week, and Nana Reba would still get her the other three times. This summer, Dawn and Taya would have hours and hours of time together, as McDermott was gone during the day, and Dawn didn't have to work until almost Taya's bedtime.

Nerves bullied their way through her. She had no idea what to do with a seven-year-old all day long.

But she'd figure it out. That had become her new mantra, and she wasn't going to let her fear of the unknown dictate her decisions. Not anymore.

"It's time," Wren said, letting the blinds fall back into place. "Are you ready?"

Dawn took a deep breath and faced her family. "You know what? I think I am ready."

She hugged her mom, and everyone exited the cabin that had been donated to her for the bride's room, leaving her to go last. Her father stood on the porch, all decked out in his black tux and starched, white shirt.

"Sweetheart." He smiled at her and placed a careful kiss on her cheek. "Let's go."

The wind tried to steal her veil, and Dawn kept a tight hold on her father's arm with one hand while she held her veil on with the other.

She sent up a quick prayer that the wind would die down, just for a few minutes, and kept moving toward the huge tents that had been set up on the north end of the drive. A huge grassy field spread before them, with the homestead on her right and the stream she and McDermott had ridden out to once way out on her left.

The wedding party started down the aisle, and the crowd stood. She caught a glimpse of McDermott down at the far end of the tent, splendid and handsome in his dress uniform. She'd wanted everything to be police-themed, and he hadn't put up a fight. At one point, he'd said she could do whatever she wanted, because for him, the prize was in gaining the wife, not putting on the wedding.

But he'd been married before. She hadn't. And as Dawn met with her mother and brainstormed with Wren, she realized she wanted a nice wedding, complete with a half white, half police blue wedding cake. And she'd gotten just that.

His daughter stepped down the aisle just like they'd practiced, an old police officer hat in her hands. Nana Reba had sewn a pillow to fit inside, and the ring was nestled there.

McDermott bent down and kissed his daughter on the forehead before taking the ring and straightening, looking for her. The bridesmaids moved, and then there was nothing between her and McDermott except the sixty-foot aisle.

Dawn managed to make it to him without tripping, noting that the wind had indeed died down to a tolerable level.

"Hey, gorgeous," he said, taking her bouquet and passing it to Berlin to hold.

Too nervous to speak, Dawn could only smile. Pastor Peters gazed at her with such love, and a keen sense of peace and comfort flowed through her.

"Look at us gathered together for another wonderful wedding!" he announced to the crowd. Everyone sat down, and he began speaking. "As humans, we're not perfect. We can strive to do a little better each day, but we'll inevitably fall short. But it is in our failures that we can learn the most."

He continued on, and Dawn basked in the warmth of his words.

"Now, I think it's time to get these two married. Don't you think?"

McDermott nodded and several people in the crowd laughed. Pastor Peters read the vows, and Dawn was able to push out "Yes," when it was her turn to pledge herself to McDermott as his companion and wife.

"By the powers vested in me, I now pronounce you husband and wife. You may kiss your bride, McDermott."

He leaned down, and she tipped up on her toes.

"You're the best mistake I've ever made," she whispered just before kissing her husband.

———

Read on for a sneak peek of the next book in this series, **THE DETECTIVE'S DATE.**

Sᴎᴇᴀᴋ Pᴇᴇᴋ! THE
DETECTIVE'S
DATE Cʜᴀᴘᴛᴇʀ Oɴᴇ

"Come on, BB, hurry it up." Kyler Fuller held the door to the cabin open with his foot, his hands stuffed full of grocery sacks. His muscles strained against the plastic bags as the horizon boiled with dark gray clouds, as thunder boomed and crashed and threatened to make the sky fall.

The eight-year-old Welsh corgi somehow got his stumpy legs up to the front porch and through the door before the rain started falling. Kyler ducked in after him, glad he'd made it to the cabin before the weather.

He'd come up last night and stacked wood in the mudroom after McDermott—his best friend and now one of his sister's husbands—had alerted him to the forecast.

Kyler busied himself with putting the groceries away, missing the way his long hair used to sway with the simplest of tasks. But he had been able to get more dates since cleaning up his appearance. Now he shaved every day, and kept his hair clipped as if he were about to enlist in the armed forces.

He worked out enough mowing lawns and moving pavers that he didn't worry about adding running to his regimen. He'd tried getting out to the summer picnics this year, the speed dating event at the church, and hanging out with his friends and brothers at the karaoke bar on the weekends.

Sure, he'd gotten some attention. But not from anyone he cared to continue a relationship with.

"BB," he scolded as the dog started licking the cabinet. "Knock it off." He chuckled as the corgi seemed to give him a smile and then went right back to the cabinet, where something must've been spilled in the past.

His phone rang, but he ignored the call from his oldest brother, instead tapping out an *I made it before the rain* in response to Milton. Since another of his brothers, Brennan, had moved to California, Milt had become Kyler's wingman.

But Kyler had had enough for a while. He'd come to the family cabin up in the hills above Brush Creek, where he planned to stay for the next few days. The fishing, hiking, and relaxing would've been better if the weather was more cooperative, but June in this part of Utah was unpredictable at best.

And "Hail," Kyler said with wonder, at worst.

The sound of the hard hail on the roof and windows upset BB, who whimpered. Kyler scooped him up and held the brown and white dog to his chest. "All right, Bread and Butter. You're fine." He chuckled as the dog shook in his arms. He set the little dog on the counter and pulled out a pound of ground beef.

That got BB to hold still, and as the symphony of hail continued to beat down on the house, he seasoned the meat with salt, pepper, and garlic powder. With the grill pan heating on the stove, harder pounding sounded from the front door.

Kyler jerked his head toward the door, his heart leaping to the back of his throat. There was someone out in this storm? This far from civilization?

"Hello?" Desperation rode in the word. More banging came on the door, and then someone tried to open it. Kyler didn't remember locking the door, but the knob didn't turn. That was when he realized he was just standing there in the kitchen, while someone was trapped outside in the relentless hail.

"Just a second!" He dashed toward the door, hoping his little dog didn't waddle off the countertop of go after the raw ground beef.

He fumbled with the lock and yanked open the door to find a waterlogged person standing there. Kyler blinked, surprised to see the curve of a woman's body inside the police uniform.

All beige, the pants ended in black boots. She wore a belt cinched around her trim waist, and when her dark eyes met Kyler's, he sucked in a breath. "Dahlia?"

"Can I come in?" she asked, her voice raspy as her chest heaved.

"Have you been running?"

"It's coming down out here," she said, still panting.

"Come in, come in." Kyler stepped back to let Dahlia Reid enter the cabin. She took off her flat-brimmed hat and let the water drip to the floor. Kyler didn't mind, but he had no idea what to do with her. He mowed lawns, trimmed bushes, and built retaining walls for a living. He didn't know what to do with beautiful, soaked detectives.

"I'm—uh—making dinner. You want something to eat?" That sounded like a good idea. Food. Water. Shelter. The bare necessities of life. He stepped past her and managed to save the bowl of seasoned beef just before BB got his snout into it.

"We have a washer and dryer here too. We could get your clothes dry."

Dahlia wandered a little closer, her boots squeaking against the hard floor as she continued to drip water everywhere. "How big is this place?"

"Pretty big," he said. "We used to come up here for family vacations in the winter."

"All nine of you?"

"Eleven," he said. "My parents came too." He flashed her a smile, glad he didn't have to explain to her about his huge family. She used to be one of the patrol officers in the Brush Creek Police Department, and she was well-acquainted with Dawn especially. His wildest sister, Dawn had gotten in the most trouble growing up.

But Kyler didn't know Dahlia Reid. He just knew *of* her, the same way she knew of him and his family.

"Do you think there might be something I can change into while my clothes go through the wash?" Dahlia ran her fingers through her hair, combing some water from the curly ends.

Kyler stared at her, sure she was a dark-haired angel straight from heaven. His mind seemed stuck on someone he'd known about but had never seen.

"Kyler?" she asked, cocking her head to the side and training those dark as pitch eyes on him.

He shook himself out of this stupor and said, "Oh, yeah, probably." The scent of a too-hot pan met his nose and he hurried to turn down the heat under the grill pan. "Let's see, um, my sisters used to sleep in the first couple of rooms just down that hall. Feel free to look around and see what you can find."

Dahlia flashed him a brilliant smile that didn't quite reach her eyes, and turned toward the hall that led to the back of the cabin. She disappeared through the doorway, and Kyler stared at the ground beef and picked up a handful of it to make burgers.

"Idiot," he whispered. "You should've gone with her to find some clothes." But he couldn't go charging after her now. He adjusted the flame under the grill pan and got the meat sizzling.

BB yipped, but Kyler ignored him. The dog's claws

clicked on the countertop and he paced, paced, paced back and forth, giving a gargled yip every time he turned.

"I know," Kyler said, keeping an eye on the arched doorway that led to the hall. "I should've gone to help her." With all the burgers on the grill, he washed up real quick and rounded the peninsula in the island in favor of approaching the hall.

"Detective?" he called, slowing his steps as he neared the first doorway that led to a bedroom where his sisters used to sleep. The noise from the hail quieted the farther he moved into the cabin, and he listed for Dahlia's reply.

"Dahlia?" He liked the way her name rolled off his tongue.

"Coming," she called. A few seconds later, the next door down opened and she came out, her fingers still working through her hair. A smile ghosted across her mouth. "I found a few things that will do."

She wore a pair of loose pajama pants the color of mint toothpaste, and a T-shirt that had a bright red U on it for the University of Utah. Both items were too big and hung off her lithe frame. She might be thin, but she was wiry, strong, and tough. At least if his brother-in-law Tate was to be believed.

Dahlia had trained Tate when he'd first come to town, right before she was made detective for the Unified Police Unit that covered several of the small towns out here west of Vernal.

And that was the bulk of what Kyler knew about her. What he wanted to know seemed bottomless, and he quirked a smile at her. "Where are your wet clothes? I'll get them going. And I've got dinner started."

"Will there be cheese on the burgers?" She stepped back into the bedroom and returned a moment later with an armful of her wet clothes.

"Of course," he said.

"Good." She smiled at him and pushed the clothes into his hands as she passed. "I love cheese."

He chuckled and followed her back into the front part of the house, where the large living room attached to the dining room and the kitchen where he'd been working spread before him.

"Make yourself at home." He went through the door closest to the bar and opened the washing machine. The cupboard above the appliance held the detergent pods, and he got her laundry started.

He paused in the doorway to find her sitting on the couch, her back to him, her fingers plaiting her hair as she hummed. The song tickled something in his memory, but he couldn't quite place it.

The scent of cooking beef met his nose and he lunged around the peninsula and flipped the burgers, the pan hissing and spitting when the juices and raw meat met the hot surface. If he let them go longer than another sixty seconds, they'd be overdone.

He unwrapped the cheese quickly and splashed a bit of water on the grill pan and placed a big lid over the burgers to get the cheese nice and melty. He hadn't had time to get any of the toppings ready, but he flipped the flame off under the grill pan and removed the burgers to a plate to rest.

He'd never had a problem talking to women, and he sliced tomatoes as he asked, "So, Dahlia, where are you from?" He wasn't sure of her exact age, but she had to be close to his thirty-five. And she hadn't grown up here in Brush Creek.

"Vernal." She looked over her shoulder. "My parents still live there." Dahlia got up and sauntered over to the counter and leaned against it. "Can I help?"

"Oh, I'm fine," he said, reaching for the head of lettuce. "Do you have siblings?"

"Nope. Just me." Her smile seemed tight around the edges, and Kyler turned away from her to get out the ketchup, mustard, and mayo from the fridge.

"Toasted bun or no?"

"It's fine as-is."

"Then we're ready to eat." Kyler wasn't sure how long the storm would last, but when he glanced out the window, it was definitely still coming down strong. "At least the hail's stopped."

"Yeah." Dahlia started doctoring up her bun and Kyler copied her.

"So why were you out here?" he asked, knifing some mayo from the jar.

"Police business," she said, her tone guarded.

"Police business?" Surprise bolted through him. "Out this far?"

Dahlia lifted her eyes to meet his, no fear or hint of

frustration in them at all. Her expression was quite unreadable and it sparked something deep inside Kyler's chest.

"Yes, out this far." Her words carried a double meaning, and Kyler got the hint.

None of your business.

Dahlia turned away and took her burger to the long picnic-style table in the dining room. Kyler wanted to ask more questions, but he wasn't sure he wanted to see Dahlia get upset. So he zipped his lips—except to open his mouth and take a big bite of his burger.

THE DETECTIVE'S DATE is available now!

The Marine's Marriage: A Fuller Family Novel - Brush Creek Cowboys Romance (Book 1): Tate Benson can't believe he's come to Nowhere, Utah, to fix up a house that hasn't been inhabited in years. But he has. Because he's retired from the Marines and looking to start a life as a police officer in small-town Brush Creek. Wren Fuller has her hands full most days running her family's company. When Tate calls and demands a maid for that morning, she decides to have the calls forwarded to her cell and go help him out. She didn't know he was moving in next door, and she's completely unprepared for his handsomeness, his kind heart, and his wounded soul. **Can Tate and Wren weather a relationship when they're also next-door neighbors?**

The Firefighter's Fiancé: A Fuller Family Novel - Brush Creek Cowboys Romance (Book 2): Cora Wesley comes to Brush Creek, hoping to get some in-the-wild firefighting training as she prepares to put in her application to be a hotshot. When she meets Brennan Fuller, the spark between them is hot and instant. As they get to know each other, her deadline is constantly looming over them, and Brennan starts to wonder if he can break ranks in the family business. He's okay mowing lawns and hanging out with his brothers, but he dreams of being able to go to college and become a landscape architect, but he's just not sure it can be done. **Will Cora and Brennan be able to endure their trials to find true love?**

The Trooper's Treasure: A Fuller Family Novel - Brush Creek Cowboys Romance (Book 3): Dawn Fuller has made some mistakes in her life, and she's not proud of the way McDermott Boyd found her off the road one day last year. She's spent a hard year wrestling with her choices and trying to fix them, glad for McDermott's acceptance and friendship. He lost his wife years ago, done his best with his daughter, and now he's ready to move on. **Can McDermott help Dawn find a way past her former mistakes and down a path that leads to love, family, and happiness?**

The Detective's Date: A Fuller Family Novel - Brush Creek Cowboys Romance (Book 4): Dahlia Reid is one of the best detectives Brush Creek and the surrounding towns has ever had. She's given up on the idea of marriage—and pleasing her mother—and has dedicated herself fully to her job. Which is great, since

one of the most perplexing cases of her career has come to town. Kyler Fuller thinks he's finally ready to move past the woman who ghosted him years ago. He's cut his hair, and he's ready to start dating. Too bad every woman he's been out with is about as interesting as a lamppost—until Dahlia. He finds her beautiful, her quick wit a breath of fresh air, and her intelligence sexy. **Can Kyler and Dahlia use their faith to find a way through the obstacles threatening to keep them apart?**

The Paramedic's Partner: A Fuller Family Novel - Brush Creek Cowboys Romance (Book 5): Jazzy Fuller has always been overshadowed by her prettier, more popular twin, Fabiana. Fabi meets paramedic Max Robinson at the park and sets a date with him only to come down with the flu. So she convinces Jazzy to cut her hair and take her place on the date. And the spark between Jazzy and Max is hot and instant...if only he knew she wasn't her sister, Fabi.

Max drives the ambulance for the town of Brush Creek with is partner Ed Moon, and neither of them have been all that lucky in love. Until Max suggests to who he thinks is Fabi that they should double with Ed and Jazzy. They do, and Fabi is smitten with the steady, strong Ed Moon. **As each twin falls further and further in love with their respective paramedic, it becomes obvious they'll need to come clean about the switcheroo sooner rather than later...or risk losing their hearts.**

The Chief's Catch: A Fuller Family Novel - Brush Creek Cowboys Romance (Book 6): Berlin Fuller has struck out with the dating scene in Brush Creek more times than she cares to admit. When she makes a deal with her friends that they can choose the next man she goes out with, she didn't dream they'd pick surly Cole Fairbanks, the new Chief of Police.

His friends call him the Beast and challenge him to complete ten dates that summer or give up his bonus check. When Berlin approaches him, stuttering about the deal with her friends and claiming they don't actually have to go out, he's intrigued. As the summer passes, Cole finds himself burning both ends of the candle to keep up with his job and his new relationship. **When he unleashes the Beast one time too many, Berlin will have to decide if she can tame him or if she should walk away.**

Go up the canyon to Brush Creek Ranch, where a community of retired rodeo cowboys are looking for love...

Brush Creek Cowboy (Book 1): He's a cowboy raising his son alone. She's a widow with a chocolate obsession. **Can Brush Creek cowboy Walker get over his losses and fears in order to build a future with Tess?**

Fall for a cowboy today in this inspirational western romance series! Journey to Montana for second chance romance, boss-nanny romance, forbidden romance, and friends-to-lovers romance among an awesome ranch setting in four full-length novels

The Redesigned Ranch (Book 1): The ranch foreman, the fiery new designer he hires, and an old flame that could burn them both... **Jace Lovell only has one thing left after his fiancée abandons him at the altar: his job at Horseshoe Home Ranch.**

About Liz

Liz Isaacson writes inspirational romance, usually set in Texas, or Wyoming, or anywhere else horses and cowboys exist. She lives in Utah, where she writes full-time, takes her two dogs to the park everyday, and eats a lot of veggies while writing. Find her on her website, along with all of her pen names, at feelgoodfictionbooks.com.

9 781638 760894